ECHO AND NARCISSUS

MARK SIEGEL

Durham, NC

Echo and Narcissus
An Aardwolf Press Book
Copyright © 2003 by Mark Siegel

First Edition

Library of Congress Control Number: 2002106069
ISBN 0-9706225-2-X

Cover art by Frank Wu

Cover design by Tammy Hildreth

Aardwolf Press
P.O. Box 14792
Durham, NC 27709-4792
www.aardwolfpress.com

For Max

Part I

New Orleans

1

There's a single boat resigning to Utopia, guy,
But no way home from here.

       —Max

At the height of her singing career, which some will say came up to Billie Holiday's rumpled ankle socks, Echo's voice was sweet breath through a straw, a straw poked up among swamp water reeds, as predators cruised the surface; a high-yellow voice that matched her tightly stretched teenaged skin, but *not* her short white hair, and most certainly not those pale gray eyes, startled and ready to bolt, eyes that did not belong in any human face.

King Z and Lady Juno first saw her in the Delphi, a photo negative wandering among the zydeco musicians on a board-and-cinder-block stage. At first they couldn't hear her; then barely could; and then Z surprised himself when he raised a hand to silence the two thugs arguing about the best place for a manicure and a blow job. The place went silent, all six odds-and-ends tables with their mismatched chairs, and their clue-less tourists who knew only that they felt a hard hand grip-ping their hearts, with just the implication of a squeeze.

Juno nodded toward the stage, and the little-girl voice rose, gained power, and soon was a woman screaming. Or so it seemed to the tourists, who were left shaken, hearing only Echo, over and over again, even later when an unappreciated one-man-band threw down his cymbals and cursed them in Creole, the second best language there is for cursing.

To Juno, Echo sounded like the little girl, half-sister and half-child, she'd never had.

To Z she sounded like a sex kitten pawing at the door from another world.

To the two thugs at their table, Fishbone (so-called because he used a boning knife) and Truck Stop (big enough to stop a . . .), Echo sounded like the perfect combination of manicurist and blow job artiste.

The little club, one of many Z owned, was a rotted-wood-and-bare-light-bulbs dive in the Warehouse District, two miles from the Vieux Carré, and one of the few places in the city that managed to be old without being historic, dirty without being authentic, run-down without being quaint. If someone had put a chicken wire fence around the bottles, which in fact Z had thought of doing, the place might have passed as a pawn shop.

When Z sent his men for Echo—that is, to the bar, because there was no dressing room, only an alley outside the door in the back marked *Privates*—Echo assumed he wanted her for reasons unmusical. Which he did, but not for himself, not in that way, not in his usual way.

He sent Fishbone and Truck Stop back to the bar, so only he, Juno and Echo sat at the little round corner table.

"Who the hell made you, girl?" Juno asked.

"God," Echo replied with a lack of conviction.

"Nah, I know His work. Besides, He mostly unmakes folks nowadays. Must have been somebody else." Juno had a spade-shaped, cumin-colored Cajun face and long, looping black curls, twisted with herb bundles, carvings, and the odd bone, all of it hanging free, like ju-ju charms from Spanish moss at Christmas.

"We're all orphans and bad guessers here," said Z. "Have a drink and tell us what you know."

"Have a drink," Juno said. "You have no place to go."

"I know." Echo ordered the same as Juno, a double bourbon with a water back, the latter of which she used to dab at the corners of her eyes when she tasted the former. Folded in a raggedy-ass armchair like a package from Sav-a-Buck, she told them she was from Baton Rouge.

"That's a lie," Juno challenged.

"Well, Georgia, originally, outside Athens. I moved to New Orleans for my career. To sing."

Juno leaned across the table and said, "You lost the baby, didn't you?"

Echo's face paled to nearly the color of her hair.

Z laughed. "Don't fuck with the witch woman, girl."

"You got pregnant and he told you he'd run away with you, so you dropped out of school and got on a bus, only he never showed up, did he?" Juno was showing off, not even looking at Echo's face now, studying her own nails as if they were tiny clipboards. "Ever think about killing yourself?"

Echo stared with her big gray eyes.

"Who hasn't?" Z offered philosophically.

"You haven't," Juno snorted. "When *you* get depressed, it's other people got to watch out. But this child here—you what, sixteen, girl?"

"Seventeen," Echo answered automatically.

"You had the baby because you figured at least your own baby would have to love you."

"That's why I killed it," Echo said. "To be free of—"

"Free of love? 'We free at last!'" Juno laughed deep in her chest, lit a cigarette, took a drag, and offered it to Echo, who took it. "Honey, that's the biggest lie you told so far, though you ain't tryin' too hard." Then she said, more gently, "You killed it how, by gettin' your old man to beat you up when you were pregnant? Never mind. You can sing a little, you know that?"

"I know that." Echo didn't cry, and she didn't direct anger

at Juno.

Z watched the two women thoughtfully. "You want a job?" he said to Echo.

Juno gave him a look.

"Singing, I mean."

"Yeah," Echo said, glancing only briefly at Z before she looked back at the table in front of Juno. Echo's strategy, a good one whenever she played with big people, was to make herself as small as possible. But anonymity, the poor man's kryptonite, failed her this time. She couldn't help singing.

Z felt in his pocket for a pen and something to write on, found neither, and pulled out a knife so wicked the folks around there probably had a name for it. "Carve your number on this table," he rumbled, handing her the knife.

"She ain't got no number, fool," Juno told him, patting Echo's slender back. "The asshole you pay to run this place keeps her money for letting her eat leftovers and sleep in the back."

Z pretended to frown; actually he didn't *pay* the asshole anything, just let him keep some of what he made.

Juno said, "You need a place to stay, child? You can stay with me."

"Why you bein' so nice to me?" Echo asked.

Juno smiled, pleased to see the girl had enough brains to be suspicious. "Same reason you sing. It's what I do."

Z ran a lot of the smaller nightclubs outside of the French Quarter, and some whores and drugs, the way a big dog runs the street he walks on. He controlled the gun trade through-out New Orleans. No formal transactions, just sniffing and pissing and then taking what he wanted without having to bite anybody, usually.

The most surprising thing about Z, when you looked at

him close up, was that he was a white man, a Caucasian who somehow had co-opted the density, the *gravitas* of a black king who had become a slave, and then a king again. He had a twenty-inch neck, hands too large and thick for normal commerce, and a sexual appetite that only Juno held in check, and only some of the time.

"The trouble with the devil," Juno told Echo a couple months after they met, "is that he keeps his bargains."

That first night, Echo rode with Z and Juno in the back of a big black car, with Fishbone and Truck Stop in the front. They left the Warehouse District, ducked under Interstate 10 and headed toward Mid City, rolling down pock-marked avenues that were still holding out against the hundred-year-old fad of electric street lights. Then the car found an even worse neighborhood, and pulled in front of a great old Regency-style house, well maintained and enclosed in wrought iron. Juno explained that no one, including the police, ever fucked with her wrought iron, thanks to Z having the place watched 24-7.

"Doesn't mister Z live here too?" Echo asked. The two women already had adopted the habit of speaking of the man as if he weren't there, or at least as if he were incapable of understanding their words.

Juno smiled and shook her head. "He just comes by to get what he wants. Never stays the night. Better for everybody that way. Fishbone and Truck Stop park out front, but they don't come in. Some boots don't ever get wiped clean."

There were a dozen rooms for just the two of them; it reminded Echo of when she worked at the Olympus Motor Inn, where no more than two of the twelve rooms were ever rented. (Though they rented only the rooms near the office, they changed the sheets in every room every three or four days, sheets dirty with a strange, gray . . . film. Not slime or dirt, more like shadow, like a trick of some outlaw light breaking optical rules.)

Because Z was coming in to do what he did with Juno, Echo slept on a funky old couch in a room on the north side of the house, a drawing room with an unused fireplace, a mantel of carved walnut and plaster columns, several over-stuffed armchairs covered in the same dark green velveteen as the couch, a jungle of potted ferns and hanging plants, and an aged but not yet tattered rug on the wooden floor. The room felt good to Echo, who was good, maybe too good, at know-ing what felt good, and she did this trick she always did to make it feel even better: she imagined herself as Juno, falling asleep on the couch after making love to Z. So she left the door to the room open, because it was her house, and she was completely comfortable in it.

Sometime during the night Echo half-woke. Moonlight through the north-facing bay windows suffused the room with soft shadows, densely jungled but playful, cast by plants and furniture. They fascinated Echo, shifting as the light out-side shifted. Gradually, she became aware of something else among them, one shadow that didn't shift in quite the same way, one that came closer.

She wasn't frightened, because she was being Juno, in Juno's house—and because Echo accepted the inexplicable as part of life—but it did *keep* coming closer. By the time it reached the foot of the couch, she was noticing other shad-ows among the shadows, and when it slid up and touched her foot, warmed her toes, it seemed . . . surprised. Echo remem-bered holding her sister's baby when it was still too young to see, and thinking, while her sister tied off her arm with a rubber cord and heated a spoon for herself, that the baby knew people well enough by their smell, and that smells ran in families, so the baby knew she was family, and was cool with family—or would be until she got to know them better. Echo didn't want to think about babies, though, so she started singing to the shadow, in her small voice, not singing words, but humming, the shadow of words. The shadow at her foot grew denser. The shadows in the shadows, pockets of density, came closer.

She didn't hear the outside door slam, though she remembered the sound afterward, and didn't see Juno come into the room, though she suddenly saw her at the foot of the couch, checking things out, concerned. She was dressed in . . . rain.

"There you are," Juno said, but she wasn't talking to Echo. She spread her arms; the rain fell from them silently, never quite striking the floor, and when she left, the shadows left with her.

2

To be sixteen is to be a casualty,
but not necessarily a victim . . .
Take the bullet like a teenager.
                              —Max

Blue flowers grew in Juno's garden, the garden in back, surrounded by willow trees, not the one on the street, where thick-thorned vines snaked through the wrought iron and seemed to come alive at night when anyone approached. The blue flowers glowed at dusk, like phosphorous under black light. Echo picked some and put them on a table in the darkened dining room, where they shone brilliantly for a few hours and then died, perhaps from too much of nature's own black light. The little shadow creatures crowded around the vase as the petals fell, and went very still when Juno entered the room. "Stop it," she said. "You'll get fat!" They slid off the table and disappeared, as if a shade had been lifted to the daylight.

Later, Echo couldn't take her eyes off the little shadows as they crept into the evening's camouflage. "I've never seen anything like that before," she said, but her voice was not truly astonished. She'd also never seen an electron or a foreign country, yet was assured those existed, assured by people smarter than she.

"They're umbra," said Juno. "Or *it* is. Umbra is one thing and many at the same time."

"Umbra," Echo repeated. "What do they eat, exactly?"

"You, of course. And they drink light beer."

"Really?"

"I'm kidding about the beer."

"When I sang to it—to them?"

"Either." Juno put two coffee cups down on the table. "You drink it black," she stated.

"If you do. When I sang to it last night, I thought it was trying to take on a color."

"It can't."

"But it seemed to be trying."

Juno frowned. "You confused them. They thought you were me. They've never gone to anyone else."

Echo smiled, and Juno couldn't help smiling back. "You can sleep in my room if you want, or stay on the couch. Or we can try to get a spare bed set up for you somewhere. But when you return tonight you should stay with me."

"Return?"

"You have a . . . date . . . with Z tonight."

"With Z? But I thought he was *your* . . . I mean, ain't you going with us?"

Juno shook her head. "Not tonight. He's going to show you a club tonight, where you'll be singing, and after that, well . . . you're on your own, child." She said it softly but resolutely, and didn't look away when Echo stared at her, continued to stare, with growing panic. Juno added, "Don't worry, child, he won't hurt you. It's just an initiation thing, into the Church. You have to see it that way."

They said no more about it, until it was time for Echo to get dressed. Juno took her to a closet full of clothes that wouldn't have fit the bigger woman, and found her a tight red cocktail dress. "You don't have much up top, but this'll show off that tight little booty. Try it on."

Echo blushed, but did as she was told, and then Juno made up her hair. "You won't need make-up, but you got to smell nice," Juno said, rooting through a forest of glass bottles without finding what she wanted. Finally, shaking her head, she selected a bottle that had stood separate from the others, and shot a spray of perfume down the front of Echo's dress.

"That's *your* perfume," Echo said.

Juno sighed. "Well, it's supposed to smell a little different on everybody."

"Supposed to."

Fishbone knocked and stuck his head in the front door, ready to escort Echo to the car. Juno pointed her down the stairs. When Echo looked back to thank her, Juno had a grim smile on her lips, like a mother whose only child has just been sentenced to a torturous death. "Remember to come to my room when you get back," she said at the last second.

Geographically, New Orleans is much smaller than it is in any other sense, one of those Escher-drawn cities defying the usual laws of time and space. Truck Stop, crammed into the driver's seat, as tight a fit as Echo's dress, his elbows up, both hands planted firmly on the steering wheel like he was trying to pull it out of his chest after being impaled, took them down shadowed streets and alleys unfamiliar to Echo. "We're meeting the King at Circe's," Fishbone said, less out of courtesy, Echo could tell, than just to have something to say.

In less than five minutes, they pulled in front of a nightclub that seemed a million miles away, but in fact was in another part of the Warehouse District. Echo couldn't help but be pleased that the place looked bigger and fancier than the Delphi, where she'd literally sung for her supper the night before. It even had its own movie house marquee over the entrance:

Circe's
We Turn Men Into Pigs Every Night

Truck Stop went to park the vehicle while Fishbone ushered Echo inside. What had looked like the main room was actually smaller than a second, attached room off to the left, with tables and chairs for close to a hundred people. To the right of the doorway was a long bar, and straight ahead were a dozen tables and then a bandstand, a real one, about fifteen feet deep, that could hold six or eight musicians. There were six fat ones up there now, tuning up without bumping into each other.

"C'mon, kid," Fish said. "You don't move, nobody's gonna be able to get in here to listen to you." Especially not Truck Stop, whose appearance in the door behind them was announced by simultaneous complaints from both door-jambs.

Z was sitting at a large table in the corner of this first room, consulting with a seventh musician, a black guitar man in a worn black suit. The suit had silver trim, and the man had greasy black hair with its own silver trim. Echo smiled at him and he frowned back skeptically.

"This is the girl I was telling you about, Orr." Z's words carried a lot less information than Orr's look. "Sit down, Sugar."

"Echo," she reminded.

He looked at her with a curious smile. "Echo," he said. "Echo. Tell Orr what you like to sing."

Echo and Orr looked at each other with blank expressions, then began to smile. "What do you like to play?" Echo asked.

So they talked about a little Billie Holiday, a little Ella Fitzgerald, a little Big Mama Thornton, singers a child had no right to know about. "Shit, don't you do no Lauryn Hill hip-hop?" Orr laughed. "Orr is all about choices."

"Only in the shower," Echo replied.

"Let's go girl."

When Echo mounted the stage, stood in her spotlight, with the sax and the trumpet, the congas and the drum, the bass and guitar/back-up singer, and sometimes just the piano, all other sound was sucked out of Circe's. Echo didn't just "do" other singers. Yes, she did their songs; so did a thousand lounge acts, singers with more technical training than Echo would ever have. But she did their voices, too, and that was all instinct, knowing how a song ought to sound. Halfway through the set, Orr caught on. He took "St. James Infirmary" out of Ma Rainey's tempo and led Echo into something more like Louis Armstrong's—and Echo became both at once. Not something in between, not a voice struggling between two disparate tempos, but a synthesis, a synergy of the two great versions.

Z sat between Fishbone and Truck Stop, puffing unfiltered Mexican cigarettes, staring and thinking, Z, who could be crushing a man's skull in his hands and still be thinking. He looked around the room at the rapt faces. A lot of idiots, smiling pleasantly, tapping their feet and fingers as they talked over the music. A few people who actually understood, paralyzed with bewilderment, knowing this was not supposed to happen here.

An hour later, Z signaled Echo off the stage, and when she didn't notice, Orr called a break. "Girl, you in the zone," he whispered.

She smiled at him brilliantly. "That's where I live. That's the only place you'll find me."

Z praised her. He gave her a double bourbon, purposefully forgetting the water back, then ordered her another when he asked for the water. "Honey, what do you believe?"

She looked at him blankly. "What am I supposed to believe?"

He narrowed his eyes and leaned across the table, his

shoulders a mountain range filling the vista. "You ever hear of Lilith?"

"Like in Lilith Fair? I can do any of those songs if I hear 'em played."

"Lilith was Eve's sister," Z told her. "The one who refused to be subservient to Adam."

"Huh?"

"The Bible left out a few things." Z waved his hands so expansively that Echo couldn't possibly see both of them at once. "For instance, where the hell did Adam come from?"

Echo reflected. "God made him?"

Z snorted. "Made man first? Would you? I wouldn't. You make man to take care of woman, to pleasure woman. Woman gives birth to man. Woman is eternal life."

"Ah," said Echo, looking into the face of something that could destroy her on less than a whim.

"I'll tell you about it. No, I'll show you," he said magnanimously.

The place he took her, another house he owned, differed from Juno's, at least as far as Echo could see, only in that the big downstairs room, the room of plants and shadows in Juno's house, was bare, bare save for the white plaster altar that looked like it had been swiped from a mausoleum, the two gold knives resting on the altar, and the dozen hooded figures waiting for them there.

Z stepped to the altar and spoke: "Lilith, vilified by Man, demonized by men, because you refused to kiss His feet, to be a mere vessel of His will, hear us, your true servants. Let us be your demons. Let us revenge you upon Mortal Man." Then he started babbling in some language that didn't even sound like a language, and the others babbled along with him. Echo, wondering if they were just faking the sounds, was too nervous to concentrate, to follow along, to maybe scat them back a bit of their babble, because suddenly Z was saying, in English again, "And grant us your sign by giving us this young woman."

When Z led her to a dais at the front of the altar, the hooded men all raised their arms in unison. Echo was waiting for them to say something about this Lilith, to chant something about her, when they all dropped their arms and Echo felt the red dress ripped from her back. As Z laid her across the altar, he mumbled something in her ear that she didn't catch. He raised the two gold knives above his head for the others to see, and his robe fell open to reveal his formidable naked body.

"No!" she wailed. "I'll do whatever you want. Don't kill me!"

Z brought one of the knives to his own throat and pricked a bulging vein; the blood flowed in a thick stream across his rock-hard pectorals and abs down to his even harder cock. Then he held the other knife to her throat and repeated the puncture. Breathing like a race horse, Echo felt her blood trickling down her neck, pooling under her bare shoulder. Z plunged his head down, sucked at the rupture, nearly smothering her with his enormous bulk.

Out of the corner of her eye, Echo was aware of the hooded figures approaching. "I can't fuck twelve guys," she whispered. "I'm a kid, for Chrissake."

"For Lilith's sake, you won't have to," Z whispered back. "Woman." He was inside her before she knew he was going to enter, splitting her apart. His hand on her mouth stifled the scream, then dropped away.

In a painful way, it was interesting. The twelve hooded figures were chanting some bullshit, she had no clue what. And when she felt Z about to come, finally, thank God, the

front door suddenly swung open. The chanting stopped, a
man at a time, sputtered to a halt. Z kept pumping, but he
looked over, and Echo, who only *thought* she'd had her eyes
shut, couldn't help doing the same.

The most beautiful blond boy Echo had ever seen, lean but
muscled, over six feet tall, was standing in the doorway, staring not at her but at Z. He looked at most a year older than
she.

"Shit," he said. "Sorry I'm late."

Echo did close her eyes this time, and, as Z exploded
inside her, she saw the blond boy.

At 2 A.M., when Fishbone unlocked the door for Echo,
Juno's house was dark, save for a pathway of glimmering
candles leading up to Juno's bed chamber. Juno lay on her
back, under the sheets, apparently asleep. When Echo's eyes
had adjusted, she realized the shadowy pattern she'd imagined on the bed covers was the umbra. They flickered briefly,
but didn't move as Echo tossed the remains of her dress in a
corner and stepped out of the brown plastic trench coat the
Lilith worshipers had given her to wear home. She slid naked
into bed beside Juno, who spoke without opening her eyes,
asked if she were okay.

"Okay," Echo said quietly, touching the bandage on her
neck. "What about you?"

Now Juno opened her eyes. "You smell like him."

"I took a shower before—"

"You know what I mean, girl. When you came in here just
now, you were walking like him. You even sound a little like
him."

"Z?"

"Not Z," Juno snapped in exasperation. "Max."

The blond boy. "Who is he?"

"Another of Z's children. Like you are now. Not *just* another one, but one of them."

"You mad at me for . . . being with Z? I mean, it's not like I had a choice."

Juno gave a thin laugh. "Once is okay. It's the way he marks you as his. Maybe it beats being pissed on, maybe not. I'm down on it. I'm like you, I don't really have much choice on that score. Just don't *like* being fucked by him, okay? No, don't even do it again." She sighed, slowed down. "If it happens again, you tell me. I got my ways of dealing with Z, ways even he has to respect."

"Thank you." Echo smiled up at the ceiling. Lines of light, thin and erratic as pubic hairs, streaked across it, never tiring of searching for something they could not yet find. "Are we going to sleep now?"

"Yes."

"Can I . . . I know I'm naked and everything, but can I hold you?"

Juno laughed and embraced her. They fell asleep, and the shadows on the bed shifted their pattern, like a kaleidoscope that's been turned, then resolved into something a little different and a lot the same.

3

Back off!
Put those itching hands back in your pockets.
These words are mine.
This is my damned poem,
the light inside my eye sockets.
                              —Max

Max ran away when he was fourteen, and stopped running when he realized no one was chasing him. Tall, with looks that couldn't last, he tried working the streets and realized he needed protection. Z didn't usually take on boys, for business *or* pleasure, but he made an exception for Max on both accounts.

A couple months after Max arrived in New Orleans (New Orleans because of an Anne Rice novel, and a truck driver who couldn't decide if he were Max's father or his mother), an elderly fag who'd used Max had moaned something about orgies and a religious cult, and Max had kicked back the twenty bucks he'd been paid, for directions to the old church on Rue Carne.

Boarded up in front, the church was deserted on the first night, but Max's instincts told him to keep trying, different hours, different nights. A week later, from the roof of the building next door, he saw stained light coming from one of the ancient chapel windows, and watched several cautious figures enter the church through what appeared to be an attached mausoleum. Max simply followed the next visitor in.

The mausoleum, Max discovered, was not so much a security checkpoint as noise insulation against the racket inside.

The boy had never seen anything like this—and he'd been fucked, sucked, and used liked a dishtowel over the past few months. The place was a madhouse. Along the wide marble hall, thirty yards on a side, people having sex with each other, or with each others, or even with themselves. People dancing. People gorging themselves. He was mesmerized by the nude and nearly nude women—the nearly nude more than the nude, actually. He wanted to instruct some of those gyrating wildly to music which, in his opinion, was not bad but might be improved on, that they didn't need to work so hard, but he learned after about thirty seconds that a beautiful woman who still thinks she has to work hard is something special.

Along the outside of the room were a dozen alcoves inhabited by marble statues, statues of saints, probably, although considering Max's religious education, they could have been any lost souls looking for a toga party. Half the statues had nude counterparts, male and female, dancing with them or caressing them or simply lying upon them—or some combination of the three. And there was, in the middle of the room, a marble altar, covered with food.

Max hadn't eaten in days. He had little money, and usually saved what he did have for cigarettes and to buy his way out of trouble when some hardass he couldn't outrun threatened to beat the crap out of him. When it came to Maslow's hierarchy of human needs, Max counted himself an anarchist. But this lunch looked free.

The centerpiece was a roast beef as big as he could have carried in both arms, which he thought about trying. Two large golden carving knives—well, not carving knives exactly, but big knives—were crossed and sunk deep into the blackened carcass. There was a lot of green stuff, which at least served as a soft landing for a few enthusiastic lovers, but the vegetables had been, in Max's opinion, kept to a discreet and appropriate minimum.

As he tried to amble unnoticed across the hall, Max felt himself being bumped by first one dancer and then another, grabbed and swung, slamming finally into a full-breasted, green-haired woman, several inches taller even than he. He paused, perhaps unnecessarily, then eased himself away from her and toward the buffet, losing his shirt along the way, but reaching the center of the room, where he quickly crammed a piece of bloody meat into his mouth. He grabbed another in his left fist as he chewed, glaring distantly out across half the room at no one in particular.

The hand that fell on his head encompassed it like a hat. When he turned, Max was staring at the chin of a man almost twice his weight. He looked up into a surprising blond face; then he stretched out his left hand and offered the meat. Z smiled.

When you hooked for Z, you either did it full time or you did specials and had a day job somewhere else in his organization. Max's job was working at one of Z's clubs, whatever they needed him for. He had little aptitude for cooking—just lacked interest. Bartending was cool, because he got to talk to people, console them, manipulate them, generally to their benefit. But it was the music that knocked him out.

He'd always known he had an affinity for music, but Max had treated piano lessons—well, any kind of lessons—as corporal punishment. But talking with the musicians in rehearsal, learning from them, jamming with them, wasn't being told what to do.

He played guitar, because no one saw the drummer, and the piano player couldn't kneel down with his crotch in somebody's face. He had a knack for lyrics, too, because, after all, he was just talking back to the music.

Perhaps by some design other than Z's, Max sat in a few times at the Delphi, played guitar, sang back-up vocals. One gig led to another, and within a few months, he was leading his own band, the Narcotics.

His musicianship was beyond his years, but what pushed him to the front of the band so quickly was his songwriting. Max's songs were about losses you shouldn't have to face, about an ironic searching without hope, about a limited grasp that always overreached. When he sang them, they were true. They bypassed the brain and embedded themselves in your heart. And it was up to you to recover.

"Love," Max said into the microphone, "is what dirty old men speak of in a back alley while they bend you over a trash can." It was his way of doing a sound check. Narc was playing this night at Circe's for the first time in months, the group having long since graduated up the scale from this particular venue. But Z had called that morning and informed him of a change of plans for the evening, and now, just as he was doing his sound check, in walked the King himself, leading by the hand some little, beige-skinned girl with short white hair. When Z gestured him over and he noticed the high sharp angles of the girl's face, the way she almost continually stretched her longish neck like a horse waiting to be startled, he thought perhaps he recognized her from one of the Lilith orgies, or a private ceremony, but he wasn't sure. Bottom line, he wasn't sure if he had fucked her yet, although the way she looked at him made him think he had.

"Max, this is Echo," Z said. "I want her to sit in with you tonight, sing a couple of songs. You can work out the details." And that was it. Z went and sat at a corner table with the manager, and Max led Echo up onto the stage.

He'd already dragged a couple of chairs up there, so he sat

down in one—just to see if she were bright enough to figure out the other was hers—and picked up his guitar. He had only a vague idea what Z wanted him to do, but he knew that was what *he* was supposed to figure out. Maybe Z had fucked her and this was her payoff (although usually Z didn't bother making deals with little girls), or maybe he wanted to find out if she actually could sing (the name, Echo, sounded vaguely familiar, Echo, echo), or maybe she did sing and Z was looking for a band to put her in (hopefully not his).

"So tell me about yourself."

"I'm from Georgia and—"

"No. That doesn't matter; that doesn't exist," Max said with finality, as if she'd never have to worry about that distant past again. He plugged the guitar into the amp and set the volume down low. "What sort of stuff do you sing?"

"Anything."

Max snorted. Usually that meant *nothing*. He looked into her gray eyes and began to play a guitar version of "Row, Row, Row Your Boat," slowly and painfully, ignored that she was just staring at him befuddled, kept staring back at her, and kept playing, his fingers twisting the notes into a Hendrix-style complaint; and he went on that way, riffing and staring, and damned if her mouth didn't open. What came out first was the high, sweet, childlike lyric, for about a chorus, but the next time through, she got to "gently down the stream," and there was something very ungentle about the words, and the third time she was screaming it, and "down the stream" meant something entirely different, like maybe, "down your throat," and "merrily" became somebody called Marilee.

"Hmmm," Max said, letting the notes trail off, but not letting go of her eyes until they were focused again, and then he smiled. He took her through a Johnny Lang song and a

Cure song and a P.J. Harvey, to which she didn't seem to know the words until he whispered them to her, and then she sang them as if she'd written them. That perplexed him, so he played one of his own, which of course she couldn't know, and he sang it to her, but she didn't try to join in, just stared at his mouth until he started feeling she was just like all the rest. Except she was good at singing. So he brought her back to some blues and R&B classics.

Z had dismissed the manager and was talking to some freak, not Fish or Truck, some wannabe Max had seen maybe once or twice, a dirty detail man. Z's eyes were narrowed into slits. Max unplugged his guitar and offered Echo a swig from his water bottle, then took her back to the drum kit where he laid out a couple lines of coke for each of them. This was not an afternoon thing to do, but he felt oddly wired, and wanted it to be because of something he was familiar with.

The girl must have at least seen other musicians snorting, but the dollar bill unrolled on her, and she had trouble inhaling, and Max wondered if she'd ever done this. Her eyes, he noticed, were bright, like mercury. He looked back across the room. Dirty Detail was gone. Max motioned with his head and led Echo off the stage and over to the corner table.

Z grunted. "All set?"

"She could use a beer," Max said, "or a Coke." He cared about her throat, anyway.

Z waved at the bartender without looking away from the two teenagers. "So what do you think?"

"She sings," Max said to Z. Then, to Echo: "You sing like everybody but yourself."

"That's because nobody ever heard of her," Z said. "But they know Ella Fitzgerald or Billie Holiday or Gwen What's-her-name. Everybody knows *them* when they hear 'em."

"I can sing like me," Echo told Max. "I bet I could . . . if you wrote the songs. Like that one you wrote for yourself, about that three-faced woman who wants to be your mother and your sister and your lover at once, but doesn't realize how you felt about your sister . . . "

Max let her trail off, wondered if she were guessing who the song was about.

Now Z eyed the two of them shrewdly. "You got this talent to be other people, Echo. Can you fuck like whoever you want, too?"

Echo held her breath a moment. "Juno told me, *Only once*, or she'd be mad at both of us." She was trying not to snivel. Maybe from the blow, there was a wet spot under her little flared nose.

"Well, we don't want Lady Juno mad at us," Z said. Echo wasn't sure he meant it, wasn't sure he didn't. "But see, if you're not being you, if you're fucking me like someone else, then that wouldn't count, would it?"

"It might count," Echo said. "If you want, I'll ask Juno if it would."

The bartender came over with a beer for Max and something that looked like a frozen margarita for Echo, as if he knew what she drank. He went to pick up a crumpled napkin from the middle of the table, but one of Z's big hands stopped him in mid-reach, and the man straightened up and went back to the bar without even a shrug.

"She lives with Juno," Z told Max. "They've become quite the pair. I hardly see Juno any more."

"Mr. Z, I just do what she tells me—"

Z silenced her with a gesture. "That's okay, you keep doing that. I need to be . . . by myself sometimes."

Max snorted, and Echo, as if in some bizarre chain reaction, sneezed. She grabbed her nose like an embarrassed child and snatched the crumpled napkin from the middle of the table, dabbed her nose with it, apologized, and was reaching for her drink when she saw what Z and Max already had seen, what it was too late not to see. A severed finger was poking straight up out of her frozen margarita.

Z took the napkin from her hand, used it to retrieve the finger. "I wouldn't drink that if I were you," he said, indicating a red stain in the middle of the pale green slush pile. "You don't know where this finger's been." He looked down at the open napkin. "Been into all kinds of pies it had no business being in." He crumpled the napkin around it and stuck it in his coat pocket.

Max knew better than to comment, and Echo was as frozen as the margarita she was staring at.

"So you two know what you're doing tonight?"

"Yeah," Max said.

Z looked at Echo for more than a couple seconds, like he was Darth Vader and could squeeze her eyeballs out of her head just by staring. "I know you and Juno talk a lot," he said, "but you're not talking about this." *This*, everyone knew, was the finger.

Echo nodded, at first slowly and then more vigorously.

Z smiled at her. "Okay. And I'll forget the other thing we were talking about. For now."

Max had no idea whether Echo actually knew the songs she was singing that night—he was pretty sure she *couldn't* know all of them—yet she had a remarkable gift of mimicry that let her get through anything. Well, not mimicry exactly, or not just, but a natural feel for where notes bend, where, like atoms in complex molecules, they each might attach to the melody's chain to make a new compound. She didn't just get through a song, but added something to it, found something in it, something she used to evoke her own feelings, or

at least to convince an audience of that. She half-convinced
Max too, and he didn't believe in anything.

They talked during a break when they were supposed to be
discussing the next set with the rest of the band. She told him
a little about Georgia, and a lot more than he wanted to hear
about the boy who had abandoned her. Max hated that, the
downloading chicks did before they went for him, letting him
know they were in the market for a replacement. And yet he
couldn't help acting concerned, couldn't help smiling the
doleful, soulful, ironic, little Max smile. Couldn't help making
people fall in love with him.

Daniel, the drummer (who would have liked to sleep with
Echo but who hadn't a clue), nudged Max and pointed to an
approaching suit. Max, hoping he could keep this simple,
looked around for Z. Fortunately, the big guy had slipped
out.

"You kids are really something," the suit said, reaching
into his vest pocket for the inevitable business card.

Max, hunched over his guitar, muscular bare arms sticking
out of his sleeveless red t-shirt, opened his (usually) green
eyes a little wide to show the stranger he was politely interested, but said only, "Thanks."

"Heard about you. This place is a bit off the usual circuit,
but I have to say, I'm not disappointed. In fact, just the opposite."

Max took the man's card, just to see if he were an agent or
a record company recruiter. As Max had guessed, he was an
R&D man scouting for new talent. "We appreciate the interest," Max said, "but our agent has us locked in pretty good.
He's the one you'd need to talk to." Max saw Daniel fold up
into himself like a sulking child. What the hell did he expect?
Partly for Daniel's benefit, Max dropped Z's name on the
guy. And because the record guy wasn't from New Orleans,

Max also gave him the name of a club owner in the French Quarter he maybe ought to talk to before approaching Z.

The man smiled at Echo, shook her hand too long so she had to lean forward and he could look down her skimpy little dress, and then retreated from her hopeful smile.

"That guy's from a real record company," she whispered when he was gone.

"Yeah," Max said matter-of-factly. "The new ones always come around. Till they learn better."

"Well maybe this one will check with that guy in the Quarter. Will he say good things about you?"

"He'll say Z broke his arm just for trying to book us into one of his clubs. Then the record guy will look for some other new band, if he's smart. There's plenty of talent out there."

"I don't get it," Echo said. "If Z's your agent, he'll make a bunch of money if you get a record contract."

It was too much for Daniel, who jammed his sticks into his back pocket and walked off toward the bar. "I used the word 'agent,'" Max said, "because the word 'Master' wouldn't have meant much to that guy. He's thinking even if we have a contract with Z, the contract can be bought out or something. But Z owns us, babe. He's not in this to make money. He's in it to control people at the most basic level." He could tell she didn't get it, so he went on. "You think rich people own poor people because they can pay them or not pay them, because they can get the poor to do shit for money. But poor people go home and they fuck their girlfriends or boyfriends, and they dream their dreams, and they forget all about the rich people. Z comes from the street, where you only own somebody if they do everything you want 24-7. If they're afraid of your smell but can't resist licking your ass. If they dream about *you*. Z doesn't want to be an employer. He wants to be a god."

Echo blinked at him. "So you can't ever record your music? You can't ever play big places?" And then, as an afterthought, "And I can't either?"

Max smiled his little smile, put a hand on her twitchy shoulder and felt the electricity run through her and back, circuit completed, electrons excited as all hell because they yearned to be lightning, even if they had no clue what it was like to explode. "Ever is a long time. But that's how it is for now."

Echo would get a lot of practice living in the "for now" over the next few months, Max guessed. The record guy would disappear, and Z, not wanting that kind of inquiry to begin with, would decide Echo and Max wouldn't play together after all, at least not "for now."

He lit a clove cigarette and stared up at his empty bandstand and tried to decide if he cared.

4

This is life after its cremation
in abasement's tanning salon.
—Max

Gray-weathered normalcy descended. The umbra grew fat and multiplied, chased each other around the rooms from floor to ceiling and, at night, played cat and mouse with the electric threads that hid in their flat world. And Echo's relationship with Juno evolved and deepened; Echo might have come to think of Juno as a sister or a mother, if she'd ever been close to either.

When Juno saw how taken Echo was with the umbra and electric threads, she dressed her up in them, and then herself. Juno truly looked like a queen wearing the robes of her elements, the creatures drifting over the surface of her body, half-circuitry, half-storm, always in sync with her movements. On Echo, though, they tended to slip and slide, swarm and flee, in jittery bunches, leaving bare spots and jumbled messes. Echo couldn't help looking like a child dressed in her mother's gown.

The deepening sense of kinship seemed strange to Echo, even stranger than the magic that surrounded the older woman's daily life. Sometimes she helped Juno by gathering herbs from her private garden or by serving tea, liberally spiced with those herbs, to the frequent guests who invaded the front parlor, guests who came with small requests for the health of a child, for the sickness of an enemy, for luck in love or business. And Juno sent them away happy, with mysterious packages and oblique advice—but only after each visitor had professed his or her obeisance to King Z.

Eventually Echo got around to asking about the magic. They were in the back garden, watering aphrodisiacal weeds with a sludge composed mostly of human excrement.

Juno didn't answer her directly. "You see what you see," she said.

"But you do it for other people too. The people Z sends here. They see it too."

"He doesn't send them here. They come on their own—to acknowledge him."

"Is helping them part of your job?"

"Like my fucking him, you mean?"

Echo blushed. "No, I meant . . . like my singing for him."

"I'm more than his consort, child. I'm his queen. Without me to keep the magic in line—"

"So it *is* magic?"

"People do what the King says for a variety of reasons. One of which is me."

"Does Z do magic too? That night at the Lilith ceremony, he said that he was like, well, a vampire."

Juno looked at her critically. "What do you believe?"

"What do I believe? Oh, you know, not much. Things happen, they have a shape, but I have no idea what they mean."

"Yes," Juno nodded grimly.

"But Z said he could fly, and drink people's blood, and live forever."

"People are people," Juno said. "And Z's a lousy historian. Lilith's not about orgies or bondage. To the extent she's about sex at all it has to be mutual. You ever see any of Z's fuck films?"

"No, ma'am," Echo assured her quickly.

"The fool makes women watch them because he thinks they'll make women horny. His Lilith religion is the same

way, a guy's version of a goddess cult. You understand what
I'm saying?"

"That he can't really fly?"

Juno sighed. "The better you see the shapes, the more you
can do with them. Most people can't do much because they
can't see much. You see a lot, but you don't understand it."

"I *don't* understand it," Echo agreed.

Juno studied her a moment. "Can you hear the traffic on
St. Francis?"

Echo hadn't before then. The street was close by, but the
garden, apparently, had shielded her from outside noise.

"Sing to me what you hear," Juno told her.

Echo cocked her head to one side. The pattern in the traffic noise was immediately evident to her, a symphony in
eight-bar blues. She began to hum and then to trill. And then
to dance. Juno danced with her, and Echo adapted to the
other woman's slower, more sultry dance. Shoulders shifting,
shoulder straps sliding off, feet pawing the ground, the two
danced to Echo's traffic song for what seemed like hours, but
was more like two minutes, a single cycle of the traffic light.
They pulled at each other and hugged each other, and fell to
the ground, side by side. Echo lay panting, staring up into the
soft, setting sun.

"Now listen," Juno told her.

As Echo's breathing slowed, her smile flattened out. The
traffic itself was now making the very music she had been
singing. She sputtered and laughed out loud.

"You can do one, but not the other, right?" Juno said.
"You can hear the music in anything, but you can't make it
sing for you."

Echo stopped laughing. "You mean I'm supposed to be
able to make things do what I want?"

"What we're calling magic is just a force of the earth. It

exists in some places more than others, and it moves around, too, sometimes regularly, like the tide, sometimes in big dramatic shifts, like an earthquake. You can't *make* it do anything, but you can ride it and channel it so people think you're in control."

"I don't . . . I can't figure it out, not even how to start."

"It's strange you have this gift you only use to sing in bars." Juno looked sad, then forced the expression out of her face. "What people *think* you can do is more important than what you can do, anyway. That's where all this started out."

Echo thought back. "So I shouldn't be afraid of the Children of Lilith?"

"You should be afraid of Z."

That night, after Echo wound up her last set at Circe's, Orr approached her and asked if she'd like to come with him to an after-hours place to check out some new music, maybe jam with some folks he knew.

"Will Mr. Z be mad about that?" she asked.

"We'll tell him we're stealing material. He always likes it when we get something for nothing," Orr assured her.

He drove them to the waterfront in his beat-up Impala, down streets even darker than the ones around Circe's. The nameless club they were looking for, a bar, really, was set out on the end of a rickety pier. It was the only lit building in sight.

Orr carried his black and silver guitar case in his right hand and gallantly offered Echo the crook of his other arm as he escorted her down the pier and then past the beaded curtain door into the smoky light, into a barrage of catcalls, alternately accusing Orr of cradle robbing and being too cheap to hire a baby sitter. A pick-up band was setting up on stage, and Orr went to confer with whomever was responsible for the

line-up, while Maggie, a heavy-set white singer in a red cocktail dress that might have fit her once, introduced Echo to
some of the musicians sharing flasks and reefer at the battered
tables. As they quizzed her about what she sang and how she
sang it, Echo felt like a common flower whose petals were
being pulled back one by one.

When the drummer's increasingly persistent banging indicated his kit was set to go, Orr, who had been tuning up on
lead guitar, moved from stray riffs into riffing on a particular
tune the sax man and bass player agreed with, and they were
off. Echo sat back and listened, the marijuana going to her
head but the electricity of the music keeping her awake. After
a while, Maggie was hauled up on stage to renewed catcalls
("White chicks can't hit the high notes!"), and did a couple
old lounge songs with a casual, relaxed scatting Echo admired. Then Orr croaked out another old standard, mopping
his face almost constantly with a ragged bandana, à la Satch-
mo. During the good-natured razzing that followed, he introduced "this little girl from Athens, Georgia, Ms. Echo."

She understood he'd set up the audience for her by clear-
ing their minds of Maggie's performance, and also with the
"little girl" line. She gave him a wink, and burned the house
down with a wailing version of "My Man."

The applause was unadulterated. More songs followed,
and more applause, and Echo knew she'd been accepted by
the musicians when they started to shout out things like,
"How'd you get Mama Thornton into that skinny little
dress?" and, "Who dat hidin' behind the bar wid da microphone?" She was about to sit down when Orr struck a chord
that seemed to surprise even him. He shrugged and smiled,
and Echo found herself crooning the opening bars of "Voodoo Magic."

A silence settled over the audience. At first Echo was

flattered, but as she sang, she grew alarmed. This was a party of seasoned pros, not a high school concert, and there hadn't been a moment of silence all evening. When she turned a quizzical gaze toward Orr, she saw that, even as he played, his eyes seemed fixed in a hypnotic trance. She swivelled her gaze around the room. *Seeing* no explanation for the silence, she closed her eyes and felt. And flinched in horror.

Something was coming up through the floor, through the cracks in the floor, although she doubted mere wood would have stopped it anyway. She perceived it as a black fog, but not just a shapeless cloud of particles; a sentient being of ethereal sinew and magical unbone. Where it touched, and it was everywhere on the floor now, people no longer moved. Even on the stage, as yet subject to no more than wisps of the evil, the musicians seemed fixed in trances, their bodies playing on while their minds . . .

Reflexively, Echo kept singing, as if this grasping for beauty were the twitching of an unconscious, perhaps dying, human animal.

She stumbled backward, climbed up on the guitar amp to get as far from the fog as she could. She stopped singing and shouted for Orr, but this seemed to have the opposite effect she had hoped for. The dark umbra quickened its advance, swirling, moving up the side of the amplifier. It surrounded Orr's ankles, and he stopped playing. A moment later, only the drummer could be heard working his snares, and soon he too was silent, one metal brush frozen in its downstroke.

In her mind, Echo screamed for Juno, reached out in a way she'd never realized she could.

"Your voodoo magic," Echo whispered in a musical tremor.

The thing seemed to hesitate.

"Your voodoo magic," Echo tried again, "makes me lose

control." Maybe not, motherfucker. The fog had definitely slowed its approach.

Echo sang out, full throttle, a capella. "Sweet black magic that consumes my soul." The fog didn't retreat, but it roiled around the base of the speaker, no longer advancing. She sang on, even as the women in her audience stood up and began a zombie-like procession through the beaded curtain; kept singing even when she heard a big motorized boat pull up next to the pier, heard muffled voices, and then a single, high-pitched laugh. Splashing sounds. From her vantage point on top of the amplifiers, she could see over the footlight glare, see the men in the room simply frozen in place.

After a few minutes, the engine noise faded into the distance. And still Echo sang, about the black magic that was trying to get under her skin. She'd hoped the fog would retreat with the boat, but something—her?—seemed to hold it there.

She'd been singing nonstop for forty-five minutes when she heard a vehicle pull up at the end of the pier. Car doors slammed, and a wailing, cursing chant filled the air. The evil cloud seemed to precipitate from the air, retreating through the floor boards. Or maybe dying.

When Juno pushed through the beaded curtain, Echo came off the stage and into her arms, unable to think of anything else.

"You can stop now," Juno whispered.

"Voodoo . . . magic . . . "

"Yes it was. Come with me now. We need to get out of here before these men wake up. There's going to be hell to pay." Juno led her out the door and hurried her toward the black limousine parked at the base of the pier. Fishbone was scrambling down off the hood, convinced that it was safe to touch ground again. Echo hurried along, but she glimpsed something in the water below them and froze. It was a fat white back, one red strap crossing its shoulder like a sword wound. Maggie.

In the distance, Echo thought she saw a few other, darker bodies, floating, bobbing, and she remembered the splashing sounds she'd heard. Juno followed her gaze, and drew her back down the pier. "The slavers throw the fat ones, the old and ugly ones, overboard. No profit in them."

She got Echo into the back seat. "The slavers aren't supposed to come over here without Z's permission. This isn't one of his clubs, but he wouldn't have allowed this." Her tone was less convincing than Echo had heard it on other occasions. "Did you see any of them?"

"No, only heard this one weird laugh. Those poor women," she sobbed. "I couldn't stop it, Juno."

"But you did, child. You saved your own life."

"By singing?"

"And by calling me."

"You heard me?" Echo asked through her tears.

"Even while I was making love to Z." Juno gave a bitter smile. "Hearing you like that means my ties to you are strong, maybe stronger than my ties to him. There's more to you than we know, girl. More than anyone knows."

Echo looked up to see Fishbone staring at her in his rear-view mirror.

"Where are we going?" Echo asked the next afternoon when Juno bundled her into the car with Truck Stop. "And where's Fishbone?" Seeing Truck Stop without Fishbone was like seeing a familiar torso without its legs.

Juno answered her: "He's gone ahead to scope things out for us."

Echo looked at her with her silver dollar eyes.

"If I thought it was dangerous, I wouldn't be bringing you."

"But it must be a *little* dangerous?"

"Everything important is a little dangerous."

Squinting out the windshield as if squeezing directions out of his impacted head, Truck Stop drove them out of the Warehouse District, past Market Street, where Juno said the best antiques were, past an incredible house once owned by Jean Lafaiete, the pirate. "New Orleans always has treated its pirates well," Juno observed.

"There's a lot of churches," Echo noted; she'd noticed most of them from the rich music she could feel as they went by. Juno told her there were over six hundred in the city. "Juno, what was that thing last night, that black fog?"

"A creature made of spirit. It was called there by someone, I suspect by one of the witches you're going to meet today, to help the slavers. In exchange, it fed on the pain they were causing people."

"Did you kill it?"

"It can't be killed. It's . . . Imagine it as a cloud, and imagine your music as wind that blows the cloud around. We can make it rain, we can even blow it back where it came from for a time. But it will never die."

They stopped on the edge of the French Quarter to let a funeral procession pass, dozens of singing and dancing men in bright blue coats, the kind that reminded Echo of penguins. Their centerpiece was an alligator the size of a hearse, tied to a cart being hauled by four boys. When it saw Echo, the beast opened an enormous yellow maw and snapped at her, its jaws crashing louder than the band's cymbals. Juno laughed and shrugged. "New Orleans is a National Park, darlin'."

Echo watched the men going into the cemetery. New

Orleans buried its dead above ground so that they could
come out to party at night, at least according to Orr. But
Echo knew the dead's idea of partying was not the same as
her own. "What are we doing here?"

"We're being picked up by that," Juno said, indicating a
carriage drawn by a white horse, standing in front of them.
The driver, dressed in full red and black livery, doffed his top
hat, revealing Fishbone's gleaming white skull.

"I thought you said he was scoping things out," Echo
complained, hiding her inexplicable unease at this develop-
ment. "This isn't scoping."

"He can scope and drive at the same time," Juno said.
"That's why Z pays him the big bucks."

As the horse and carriage headed into the French Quarter,
they passed an ancient cemetery, so packed with mausoleums
and crypts it looked like a warehouse on a horror movie lot.
Juno explained that the crypts had to be above ground because New Orleans was six feet below sea level at its highest
point. "This city starts below ground," Juno told her, "and
then it goes deeper. Stories about the gods living on top of a
mountain? Bullshit. Who wants to live on top of a cold, rocky
mountain?"

Echo tried to ignore what she was hearing from the direction of the cemetery, from deeper down than six feet. "We're
not going in there, are we?"

As they passed the front gate, Juno pointed to a sign that
read *St. Joe II*, and in smaller print, *Do Not Enter After Dark
or In Groups of Fewer Than 15*. She said, "This is a lousy place
for a meeting. All those teenage gangsters from the project on
the other side of the cemetery run around in there. You never
know who's spying on you."

"We're going to a meeting?"

Juno smiled. "You wanted to learn how magic works

around here. You are about to meet the two most powerful witches in New Orleans. The other two."

"Are we gonna dance around naked in the moonlight?"

"People do that every night in the Vieux Carré, cher. This is strictly business. Z and I are not exactly on friendly terms with these two and their employers. You couldn't even put Z in a room with Jinx and Madame Herod without bloodshed."

"You said this wasn't dangerous."

"We'll be safe. This meeting we're going to is on sacred turf."

"So everything between you three . . . witches . . . is copasetic?"

"*Copasetic*? You got that word from Max, didn't you? Don't use bullshit words like that around me."

"What's wrong with Max?" Echo pouted, not even realizing Juno had changed the subject.

"Oh, there's no more wrong with him than there is with a rushing river, or a great big beautiful eucalyptus tree . . . until you fall into it or out of it."

Echo thought about Max as a rushing river, and shivered all over.

Juno sighed. "Max can never give you what you want. No one knows that better than I. We'll discuss this later. We're here."

"We're here?" Echo had assumed they were slowing for traffic, en route to a secret castle or a haunted house, but she now saw that Fishbone had drawn up behind two similar carriages. Fishbone got out of his seat and came around to the sidewalk to let them out. A big stone archway stood just to their left, and a sign over it announced Pat O'Brien's.

"Pat O'Brien's?" Echo said. "Pat O'Brien's is sacred? Pat O'Brien's is a tourist trap! I heard about it all the way back in Athens. Mikey, that boy I told you about?" (She knew she hadn't exactly told Juno about him, but The Boy Who Had Deserted Her had been the topic of a number of conversations.) "He had this big glass from Pat O'Brien's from when he came to New Orleans with a couple of his friends. He tried to use it for a pencil holder, only it was too tall, and he always got his hand stuck in it trying to get out one pencil."

As they passed under the archway into a large, cobblestone courtyard, its walls covered with wisteria, Echo realized her description of the glass had been unnecessary. Everyone at every table had one, more often than not filled with a reddish liquid called a Hurricane. She looked around at at least twenty people who might have been Mikey. It saddened her to realize how many good-looking assholes there were in the world.

"Walk behind me," Juno cautioned, heading them toward a corner table occupied by two very unMikeyesque characters, "and don't look either of them in the eye unless I tell you to. You won't see Fishbone, but he'll be watching our backs."

A woman whose long white hair, restrained only by a red headband, blended almost imperceptibly into her flowing white cotton and lace dress, stared fiercely at Echo, who momentarily forgot her instructions not to look anyone in the eye. She glanced at the other creature, an amazingly tall black woman in plumes and gold jewelry. Her peculiarly jutting face, and her Adam's apple hidden behind a multi-colored silk scarf, told Echo this might actually be a man.

The table at which they sat, a plastic patio table with a big green umbrella stuck through it, made Echo feel she was the least conspicuous piece of fruit stuck around the rim of a fancy drink. Apparently, though, she was not inconspicuous enough. "Who the hell is this?" the drag queen hissed, jabbing a sword-length fingernail at Echo. "We decided no seconds." The huskiness in his voice, though well concealed, confirmed to Echo's perfect ear what she had suspected.

"If Z is breaking the rules at this point," the white witch observed, "it hardly bodes well for any negotiation."

"Echo is here precisely to show our good faith," Juno insisted. "She is my adopted daughter, a complete innocent, as you can see for yourselves."

Echo had grabbed a tall glass when the drag queen's sudden movement had nearly toppled it, and was examining its watery, Kool Aid-red contents. She looked up on cue with her wide silver eyes abulge.

"Take a sip, child," the white witch demanded.

Juno nodded, and Echo did as she was told. The Kool Aid had a hundred-horsepower kick that burned her throat and made her eyes water.

Taking the glass from her, the drag queen stirred it twice, and held it up to the light. With a noncommital grunt, she handed the glass to the white witch, who also stirred and examined it before setting it back on the table in front of Juno. Juno took a sip, stirred the glass, and set it in the midst of the three.

The drag queen reached up to his face and, when his hand came away from one shut eye, he dropped something into the glass. Echo tried to believe she was witnessing a cheap parlor trick, but the pupil of the eye in the Hurricane expanded when it looked at her.

They all stared at the glass. Echo thought she saw small worms drowning in the red pool and gagged at the memory of her burning sip, but when she looked again the water had stopped swirling and the liquid was clear. The drag queen was blinking a red tear and had two eyes again.

The white witch looked at Juno thoughtfully. "So you've come to offer her as a sacrifice?"

Juno stilled Echo's panic with a glance. "No, merely to

assure you that Z intends no violence here today. Obviously I don't bring the child if there's danger—at least from our side."

"She is no threat, but how do we know Z gives a damn about the kid?" the drag queen sneered wickedly. "He eats girls like that for lunch, and then really eats them for dinner."

"Because she is mine," Juno said, and that silenced them. They accepted that Z wouldn't cross his queen.

A waiter brought more Hurricanes. Echo hadn't drunk much alcohol—she was too young to be served legally, and, although the musicians often shared sips with her, and the bartenders at Circe's would have been glad to bend the rules, Echo generally abided by Juno's cautions. But these Hurricanes tasted like Kool Aid, and weak Kool Aid at that. The initial high octane burn she'd felt must have been from something the witches had put in the drink, she rationalized.

For her own reasons, Juno let her drink. While the witches talked about ending the slave trade, Echo looked into her Hurricane, sloshed it around a bit, and tried to imagine those old slave ships from her mother's stories sinking into a scarlet sea. She hadn't thought of her mother in a very long time, of her mean and pointless death, and a minute later she was crying to herself, thinking of her mother, and of Maggie and the other women she'd seen drowned the night before.

Juno reached out and touched her shoulder, and Echo felt a cool current unwind itself from the back of her neck down her spine, as if she were being held in sure arms on a perfect night. "If Jinx gives up his slave trade," Juno said, "I personally guarantee Z will keep the amnesty."

The other two were very much looking at Echo. "And you'll give us this child as assurance?" the white witch said finally.

Something in her words was a reaching out, a reaching out

toward Echo, until Juno's words slapped it away. "No! I said we leave the girl out of this. I will give you something of myself." She removed an amulet from around her neck and handed it to the white witch.

The drag queen, sitting back in his chair, his arms folded across his skinny chest in a very unladylike manner, whistled. "You welsh on that, and Z'll never touch you again."

The white witch looked from the amulet back up at Juno and nodded. In turn, she unwound a small charm from her hair and gave it to Juno.

The next thing Echo recalled was being helped to her feet by Fishbone and half-carried back across the cobblestones to the carriage. As the horse plodded back toward the graveyard, she managed a sigh and looked up at Juno, on whose shoulder she was half passed out. "They wanted me, but you wouldn't let them have me," she smiled, touching Juno's sleeve with a grateful hand.

"Greta would have figured out you weren't my child, even in the sense we meant it, as soon as we were separated and you began to take on her characteristics."

Echo stuck out her lower lip. She had a lot of experience with people who pretended to care but didn't, and little experience with the opposite. "Then why'd you bring me in the first place, if you didn't ever plan to let them take me?"

"To make what I gave them seem even more important than it was," Juno smiled.

"That necklace? What was in it? I mean, what does it do?"

"It contains my youth," Juno replied. Her eyes became distant, and she would say no more.

They passed a pier on the Mississippi, where a small coven of women were making offerings to the river they knew as the goddess of love, beauty, and wealth. The river was impenetrably brown and, to Echo's eye, did not look to be in a re-sponsive mood.

Along the quay, where another group of women had gathered at sunset, Juno apparently recognized someone and had Fish pull over along a weather-beaten wooden pier. The women greeted Juno with reverence, and one, silver-haired, in a faded gingham dress, approached the carriage as if in supplication.

"Still looking for love in all the wrong places, Mary Beth?"

At first Echo thought Juno was quoting the old country song, but Mary Beth nodded. "It's moved again."

Juno looked out across the muddy brown water and said to Echo, "What do you hear?"

Echo listened apprehensively to the rush of the river, then to its sub-tones, to the friction of the water against the banks and the bottom, the piers and the boats. She heard other things in the water, living creatures, she supposed, and then something different, something that reminded her of Max, very distant, toward the far shore and upriver from the pier.

She pointed.

Juno smiled again. "Yes, it's moving."

The carriage started up again. "What did you hear?" Juno asked. "Was it something in the river?"

Echo thought about that. "Two things. Both were in the river, but only one was like a *thing* in the river."

"That thing, do you think that was love?"

Echo shook her head. "No. It was . . . a living thing, not like a person or a dog or a cat, but living. It was . . . eating the other thing, but 'eating' isn't right either. More like what your umbra does."

"And the other thing, the thing that sounded like love?"

"The other thing I heard was the river itself, moving . . . around itself."

"Do you know what the physicists say about gravity? That

it is not a force making things move, but a distortion in space-time that makes things appear to move in unusual ways. That's one way of understanding magic. It is a quality of life that distorts the flow of reality."

Echo thought of Max, of being pulled toward him and of being pushed a little bit away at the same time, and wondered if she could learn to ride this magic so that it brought her closer to him. She closed her eyes and tried to abide the jolting of the carriage ride. "What did you mean before when you said nobody knew better than you why Max couldn't give me what I wanted?"

Juno was silent for a minute, then said softly, "Z and I are devoted to power, Echo. Different kinds, so we can coexist, even help each other. But I am as ruthless as he. Don't ever forget that."

5

I dance these halls
without a partner
my best friend my only foe.
    —Max

Max was surprised, and, okay, yeah, pleased when he heard
Echo was to appear again with Narc, even if only for one
special engagement. Narc was breaking in a new drummer,
Daniel having made a run for it, probably to the west coast,
after watching Z destroy one too many opportunities for a
real career. The new guy had come over from a Cajun band,
and could play anything, as long as you didn't mind it sound-
ing Cajun.

It would have been a good idea to rehearse with Echo, but
Z's orders were to just play the gig, period, and in fact, Truck
delivered Echo to the front door personally, just before they
were to start. As Max came forward to greet her, Fishbone
appeared with a black leather ju-ju pouch, and Echo dropped
something into it. "You'll get it back to me tonight?" she
asked as Fishbone tightened up the pouch. "Z said it was just
for a little surprise."

Fishbone looked at her. "Big Man's full of surprises. Don't
you worry your little . . . Just you two go make music like
you never did before."

And they did. The house was packed, got more packed as
the night went on, people crammed together like neutrons in
a reactor, and Max's electric guitar drew them into a current
that pulsed and throbbed to a critical mass, and held it, held
it until you didn't think it was possible to restrain the explosion any longer. That's when he and Echo did their duet

of Max's song, "Life's Little Pretenders."

Like a lot of Max's stuff, "Pretenders" was both manic and depressive, with a heavy bass line and a frantic guitar. In the duet, Max started out fast and brutal, Echo slow and halting, but by the end of the song they had switched. They finished the last chorus together:

we are all pretenders at this dance
who never hear the music
we break in midstep, in midglance
see the others in their lost flapping
one hand clapping,
the other clenched to abuse it,
and we resume it

There was dead silence from the band on the last phrase, just Max's and Echo's voices asking each other the same un-spoken question: Is it worth it? There was dead silence from the audience as well, and then pandemonium mushroomed out.

"I only wish Juno had come," Echo smiled later, as the band trooped into the back room to towel off and rehydrate.

"She won't come, ever, when you're playing with me," Max told her.

"Why not?"

"Why do you think?"

"But . . . " She didn't finish the thought. "Z came."

"Is that a good thing?" Max laughed. "Besides, he left as soon as we got started."

"Oh." Echo looked perplexed. "He said to be sure to tell Juno she missed a big show. To be sure to tell her that he said that."

"Then you'd better tell her," Max sighed, suddenly anxious

to get to the post-show party, where he could stop thinking and let his body call the shots.

Bodies had always littered the bad end of Canal Street. But those were just tourists and independent kids who hadn't learned respect for the "older" generation of twenty-year-old thugs. Now, familiar faces were showing up minus an ear or an eye—or not at all.

There was a war going on, and now, as the Little Tramp drove Max down Canal in her pink Beetle, he wondered why Z would have summoned him, dragging him away from hot, tasty beignets and coffee at the Café du Monde.

War was not Max's thing. He had killed a man for Z once, but it hadn't been interesting, and he'd been given to understand it was a one-time job, one of his "special assignments." All in all, Max *would* rather have killed the nasty old guy than fucked him, but it was a close call.

"I can't believe Z'd let it go this far," the Little Tramp complained to Max.

The Tramp was ambitious, had made certain investments with the tips she'd managed to hide from Z, or which Z had let her hide so far. She was concerned about the impact of the war on her properties, which were mostly made of wood in need of a paint job.

Max enjoyed his clove and smiled out the open passenger window at a mother on the street wheeling twin toddlers.

"I mean, you weren't there," the Tramp continued, "when Z jumped out of the car and ripped Sativa's head off right in front of Zulu. And then he whips out that giant pecker of his and fucks her neck. That was over the top, even for Z."

"It was just a swan, for Christ's sake! A bird!"

"But Zulu was just walking—"

"Zulu had it coming. Parading his weird-ass pet around on

Z's turf was an act of aggression. It was getting in Z's face. Like if you saw some other woman straightening the tie I don't wear, maybe giving me a little peck on the cheek. It's not like she's fucking me, right?"

"The hell it's not." The Little Tramp adjusted her bowler and twitched her fake brown mustache—brown, though the straight hair that hung over the shoulders of her shabby tuxedo jacket was blond.

If Hitler were a five foot, badly dressed stripper, he'd be driving this car, Max thought. He said, "If you wore pants, your ass wouldn't stick to the seat and you wouldn't be so anxious to declare war."

The car pulled up by a fire hydrant in front of Circe's, where a huge fat man with an enormous sandwich in one hand and a large semi-automatic pistol conspicuous in his other stood guard. "You can't park here," Max told the Tramp. "That's Fishbone's fire hydrant."

"I'll keep the engine running." She smiled sweetly, pumping the clutch just a tad so the car jumped as Max was half out the door.

"Yo, Po Boy. Don't hit me with that sandwich, man," Max said as he went inside. He took the wooden stairs up over the club to the apartment/office Z kept there. It was one of a dozen all-purpose rooms where Max had been called to meet the boss over the years. He knocked on the door, waited for Z's command to come on in.

And there she was. Echo. Naked.

It was a shabby office with a table instead of a real desk, no sign of a bed or a couch. Z was wearing a red condom that covered barely half his dick, and cowboy boots. Max had heard he only took off those boots when he was with Juno, who despised them.

"You remember Echo." Z held her off the ground in two

hands, like Exhibit A.

"Yeah." Max tried not to look at her, and she tried not to look freaked, not easy when a big guy is holding you by the back of the neck and your ass.

"Take her back to Juno's."

"Okay."

Then Z slammed himself into her. Echo's soundless scream was heard by dogs for miles around. "In a minute," he added with a grunt.

Great, Max thought, because taking her now, with your dick still in her, might present a bit of a logistical problem. He watched the big man fuck the little girl-woman, wondering if he had time for a clove cigarette. Z was mumbling something about wanting her to fuck like Madonna. That seemed unlikely to Max. Echo was stretched out along the razor edge between pain and something else, something worth living for, maybe. He tried to read her face as he took a clove from his pack of Djarum Specials. He knew about rape, about what you thought about to survive when it was happening, but that didn't seem to explain Echo's open-mouthed groans, the taut lines of her neck and face. It looked as if she were rising from water to take an enormous breath but then continuing to rise, right up into the sky. Hers was a transcendent agony, agony being made into something else.

Z's cowboy boots scraped across the wooden floor as he laid Echo down on the table and began to pump her even harder. Her cinnamon arms stretched straight out over her head, and discovered the Glock 9 that Z must have left there. Max wondered if Z had done that on purpose, wondered if the Glock were loaded, if Echo knew how to fire one. Like a lot of his wonderings, all this was purely hypothetical. He knew she'd never shoot Z.

Max put Zippo to clove, and Z, finished with Echo, said,

as if he'd just laid down a book, "Light that for me? What is that, one of those funky-ass teenage things? Shit, why don't you just roll dirt and smoke it?"

Max found a tin of little cameo cigars on an otherwise empty bookshelf, lit one of those for Z, and handed it to him, trying to keep a sanitary distance from the enormous drooping cock that was about to lose its soggy red hat. Echo lay exhausted on the table, her legs spread wide apart, looking vacantly at the two men until Z told her to hurry up and get dressed. "Who drove you over here?" he asked Max.

"L.T."

"The Tramp? Send her up."

"Then how do I get Echo back to Juno's?"

"You still don't have a driver's license? Probably she don't either," he said, gesturing toward Echo, who was pulling a short purple dress over her thin frame. "Fucking kids."

Max shrugged. "I can drive if I have to. But it's L.T.'s car. Where're Fish and Truck?"

"They're busy. Which reminds me: take that Glock. Hang around Juno's for a while."

Max pondered that order but said only, "What about L.T.'s car? She's got a show in an hour. She's already wearing her costume."

"She shouldn't be driving around like that. The upholstery marks up her ass. Very unappealing. Send her up and take the green machine parked out front." Z produced a single key, Max didn't want to think about from where. It *must* have been on the bookcase the whole time.

He held the door open for Echo, then followed her down to the street, past Po Boy, who was talking to the Tramp, who was ignoring his big fat ass. She was still behind the wheel of the Beetle. Max told her to shut it off, that Z wanted to see her. She reached one surprisingly muscular arm through the window, grabbed Max by the t-shirt, and pulled him into a long, hard kiss on the mouth.

"I am not letting him tie me up," she told him. "My wrists are sore today." Then she got out, slammed the door of the Beetle, ignored Po Boy some more, and wiggled her butt up the stairs. "And no gags. Definitely no gags," she yelled down.

The green Jaguar right in front of the Tramp's Beetle was new to Max. It might be stolen, might be borrowed; either way Z probably planned to keep it awhile, a big, fancy car like that. He might not use it much himself, too conspicuous, but it would be great to park in front of his clubs. Except that, as soon as Max opened the door for Echo, hoping his courtesy would help her feel a little less shitty, a little less like a slab of meat, he realized the car would have to be aired out. It reeked of blood and shit. With a sigh, Max slid the key into the ignition, lowered all four electric windows, and turned on the air conditioning full blast.

Echo sat primly in the passenger seat, hands folded several inches above the hemline of her recently pummeled lap, apparently unaware of the stench. Maybe she thinks all Jaguars smell like this, Max thought. He also thought of asking her to take off her soiled panties and hang them from the rearview mirror like one of those scent strips you got from the car wash, but decided it would be cruel under the circumstances.

He adjusted the mirrors and the seat height, put on his seat belt, and carefully pulled away from the curb. Max was an infrequent driver, having taken up with older women who had cars and licenses back when he was too young to legally have any of the three.

"So how's the music coming?" he asked Echo.

Without moving a muscle in the rest of her body, Echo turned her head toward him and stared. Then she burst out in a convulsion of laughter. Max laughed too. "It's okay," she said finally. "It's something. I wish I could sing with you again, though. Last night was . . . I felt . . . " She couldn't say it, and her voice trailed off.

"You felt like yourself for a change," Max nodded. "At least in the second set, when we were doing the originals."

"Oh, Max, you gotta write me a song. I can be better with you than with anyone." She paused, said, "If only he'd let me sing with you more."

"That'd be cool," Max nodded. "Maybe he'll change his mind about that when this little war is over." He'd been wondering why Z had relented on that prohibition, even for the one night, thought maybe he had just witnessed his answer a few minutes ago, up in Z's office, and that Z had brought him there to see it just so Max wouldn't think the old bastard was getting soft.

Apparently Echo was thinking about something else entirely: "War?"

"It's either already started or about to start. See the way some of these buildings are boarded up?"

"A war between who?"

"Z is one King, and this freaky little albino named Jinx is another, and Madame Herod is the third. For the most part, Z controls guns in the whole territory, Jinx runs slavery and prostitution, and Madame Herod oversees drugs. And they all have their own witches, the 'Three Sisters.' They're not really sisters; in fact they aren't even all women, but that's what they call themselves."

Echo bit a knuckle. "So that's who those witches were." She told Max about the meeting she'd been to at the sacred sanctuary of Pat O'Brien's. "But there's not going to be a war," she told him, "because they all promised."

Max gave her an astonished look. "If you believed those

three, you were the only one there who did." He lit a clove to
kill the stench in the car, persuaded Echo to take one for the
same reason.

"I trust Juno," Echo announced, exhaling into the windshield. The air conditioner blew the smoke right back in her
face.

"That's a mistake." There was an earnestness in his voice.

Echo turned toward him. "But she's never lied to me. And
she and that other witch wanted the slave trade to end."

"Sure," Max shrugged. He turned off Canal Street, deciding to cruise the Garden District to Juno's. "It's bad for
business when Jinx kidnaps the daughter of some rich white
people and they send the cops down here looking for her. But
Jinx ain't about to give that up without a fight."

Echo was about to mention the amulet Juno had given to
the white witch when Max added, "Besides, that ain't what
this war's about. Maybe they'll say it's about slavery to make
it seem legit on the street, but it's about Z wanting more
power. He and Jinx are always bumping up against each
other. Z offed Jinx's favorite boy whore last month just to
prove he could. So Jinx sends Zulu down here to parade
around, show folks he's not afraid. Only Z sends *him* pack-
ing." He decided to leave out the graphic details about what
Z had done to Zulu's pet swan, considering where Z's pecker
had been most recently. Well, more recently.

"But Juno wouldn't lie to the other witches. At least not to
the old white lady," Echo persisted.

Max smirked as best he could without losing the clove.
"Look, you don't get power down here by being chosen
prom queen. Juno *has* power and she's not afraid to do what
it takes."

"She's been so nice to me—"

"You know how Z came to power down here, how he

became one of the Three? There was a guy before him, monster-sized dude they called Titan, made Z look small. He was mean as shit, but not as smart as Z. First time anyone saw Juno, she was just a kid, around your age, but she had abilities, and got herself adopted by Titan's witch. Maybe Titan was thinking he'd like to have a replacement available, something younger, in case he got tired of the old witch, or maybe the old witch herself figured she could use Juno as a secret ally against Titan, because this new kid, Z, who had just become Titan's go-to guy, had potential. So she's humping Z on the side, and she's training Juno, and one day Juno brings home this big old black dog she says she's gotta have as a pet. Titan and his witch say okay, because the dog looks so old they figure it's about to die. But over the next year, it doesn't. The dog is weird. People say its shit talked."

"You mean, like it barked?"

"No, words, human words. I don't know if it was trying to keep from being stepped on, or what. That's not the point. See, instead of the *dog* getting sick and dying, Titan develops a brain tumor and the witch gets breast cancer, which is never supposed to happen to a witch, because they're covered against that shit by all their magic. Wardings, they call 'em. All the witches have themselves and their houses warded, but in this case, the dog was already in the house. So Titan and his old lady get sicker and sicker, and the dog starts looking younger and younger, and one day Z shoots the dog, out of respect to Titan, he says, and Titan and his witch die the same day. And Z takes over the territory with Juno as his witch."

Echo's gray eyes were wide. "You think Juno did that? Betrayed her own teacher?"

"I am so rolling my eyes," Max grinned. "Maybe that's just the story they tell when you ask why Z and Juno don't live together. This way, no one can get them both with the same shot. Look, these are power people. Doesn't mean Juno doesn't have a soft spot for you when she sees that sad look in your big gray eyes. But don't ever forget they're also this other thing." He made sure nothing in his voice, his expression, would tell Echo how hard-won this knowledge had been for him.

When they rolled up across the street from Juno's, Max declined to come in. Echo got out, and Max sat in the front seat, the window open because of the smell, the Glock in his lap, mostly because it was more interesting to play with than his lighter. He wondered if you could light a cigarette by holding the tip next to the barrel of the gun while you fired, and he wondered why Z had sent him here, since Z *had* to know about him and Juno. And he wondered who might show up, assuming there was actually some point to his being there with the Glock.

He popped open the glove compartment to see what other toys might turn up. Legitimate, up-to-date registrations didn't often come with Z's cars, but sometimes it was amusing to see who the previous owner had been.

This time it wasn't amusing.

6

Destruction is an art,
and art is the antithesis of destruction.
— Max

Juno peered through a slit in the thick brocade drapes, a slit that disappeared as soon as she stepped away from the window. The room seemed dark for this early in the evening. "Where did that car come from?" she asked.

Echo could repeat lies but wasn't very good at making them up herself, and no one had prepped her. Only later would she realize that that was because she was *supposed* to blow it. "Where did the car come from?" she repeated dumbly. She looked around for the distraction of the umbra, but none of the shadows came to greet her.

"It came from Z," Juno declared, exasperated. "But where did *he* get it?"

"It was parked . . . " Echo began, but then faltered, fearful of what she might have to reveal next.

Juno scowled. "It was parked in front of whatever shithole he took you to to screw him."

"I know you told me never again, but he—"

"Shut up." Juno paced into the dining room and Echo followed. The umbra were nowhere to be seen, and the electric threads in the ceiling were flickering nervously. "I know he forced you, and then he stuck you in that stinking car, but he did it for a reason, and I want to know what it is." Her face looked drawn when she turned back to Echo. "I need to know." She put a hand on each of Echo's shoulders and peered into her eyes. "He did this to confuse me, to distract me. He's taken Fishbone and Truck Stop away with their car, and he's left that thing out front to keep me here."

"He said they were busy," Echo offered helpfully.

"Busy doing what?"

"That's just that boy Max in that car out front. If you need to go someplace, he ain't that bad a driver, even though he don't have a license."

"I know he's there. I can smell him. Z sent him because he knows I'll never get in the car with him. And I smell somebody else on you too."

Echo tried to shrink back, but Juno held her by both shoulders. "I didn't want to, Juno. King Z made me go with him last night, after the show. He wanted me to pretend to be all these other people and—"

"Not him!" Juno was practically shouting in her face. "Who else was in that car with you?"

"Nobody, Juno. I swear!"

Juno looked at her own hands holding Echo's shoulders and suddenly pulled them back. "What is wrong with me? There's something going on and I . . . I can't . . . "

"Maybe we could have some green tea?" Echo suggested. She was near true panic herself. She had believed Juno would always know what to do, would always take care of her, and now she knew she somehow had betrayed Juno. She knew because she had seen what Juno had seen before she pulled her hands away. "Where are the little shadows?" she asked, to get this thought out of her mind.

"They're hiding. They were gone this morning when I woke up. So was the black car. Z has done something terrible, and he's left me out here, and apparently you too, after using us both one last time." Juno stopped when she said this, struck by the obvious. "He let you play with your precious Max again last night. In return for just fucking him? He could take you any time he wanted. What deal did you make with him?"

Echo sank down at the foot of the staircase so she wouldn't be tempted to look upstairs. "He said I was supposed to tell you he was at our gig all last night, when maybe he wasn't." She started to cry.

"That's a smoke screen. The bastard was giving you a message. But there's something else!" She dragged Echo to her feet in a single easy motion, as if she were made of straw, drew the girl close to her, sniffed at her, looked into her eyes. Echo saw the crow's feet at the corner of Juno's eyes crackle with blood-lightning, saw her face starting to crease with age and care, like the earth itself threatening eruption. And she couldn't help looking down again at Juno's newly wrinkled and spotted hands. Juno followed her gaze, and with a scream tossed Echo aside and ran stiffly up the stairs to her own room, Echo following, dragged up those stairs against her will, yet by her will.

Juno was standing, leaning with both hands across her dressing table, looking at the charms hanging on leather chains from the big mirror. Finally she took one of them and held it up to the light. Then she looked in horror and disbelief at Echo. The lightning threads gathered above her head like a mother ship about to disappear into the clouds.

They both heard a car pull up out front, heard its doors slam, but neither broke eye contact. Finally Echo spoke. "He said he just wanted to look at the real one for a minute, to make a present for you. And he'd give it right back. He said if I just replaced it with that and brought it to him for a few minutes, I could sing with Max, and—"

"God damn you both!" Juno hissed, flinging away the fake charm, the charm Echo had hung there when she'd "borrowed" the white witch's charm for Z.

"I didn't know," Echo pleaded. "I wouldn't betray you! I

thought I was helping—"

"By lying to me? How could you of all people—?"

There were shouts outside now, and more doors slamming, and then silence. And the house trembled. Echo heard a shingle break loose from the roof and smash on the pavement below.

"I . . . I just wanted to sing with Max."

The house groaned around them, as if being pulled apart a plank at a time. Echo heard a wailing sound, and felt something else, not a sound exactly, more like a wind that was not made of air, like a wave felt underwater, pushing her back, until she literally stumbled and fell. Juno roused herself into a fury. "Max! You just wanted to . . . I told you to stay away from him! He can't love you. He couldn't even love me!"

"Maybe he just needs someone more his own age who—"

"He can't love you because he's cursed."

"Cursed?"

"Because *I* cursed him! If he couldn't love me, he couldn't love anyone, not ever. Do you understand, Echo?"

"Not ever?"

"Stop repeating me, you brainless idiot!" Glass shattered in the front door below. With a crash, the door itself gave way. "Or better yet," Juno hissed, turning to look into her mirror, "*only* repeat. From now on, as I see my image in this mirror, you will only echo back what others say to you. You've destroyed me, all because you couldn't think for yourself. So you'll never speak for yourself again!" Juno picked up a sacrificial knife from the dressing table and turned toward Echo, who now saw the umbra, roiling out from behind the bed, the chest of drawers, the sofa, streaming up in confusion.

Feet pounded on the steps outside. Juno ignored them and raised the knife, just as something marble-sized rolled under the door right toward her. She glanced down at it, cursed, and smashed it flat with one foot. Then she snatched a small glass vial from a chain around her neck and took another step closer to Echo.

Echo heard a scream, heard the door behind her crash open. Before the knife could descend, an enormous feathered spear struck Juno full in the chest. She hit the floor backward, blood pouring from the rip in her body, even as Echo rushed to her side.

Like broken branches in the wind, Juno's hands trailed around her, drawing a circle of blood around the two women. "You're cursed, child," Juno whispered, "you and that bastard Z." Echo was looking down at the small glass vial, smashed and leaking a familiar, viscous fluid, when Juno spat her last life's blood on her.

Echo started at a horrendous whooping sound. Zulu, the transvestite witch, stood in the doorway, bare-chested except for a metal brassiere, his naked arms raised to the ceiling. "It is done!" he yelled jubilantly. His face was painted with red and white streaks and one eye was entirely closed.

Another man appeared in the doorway, a big-muscled, t-shirted mulatto with a machete. He looked from Juno and Echo to Zulu. Neither man seemed to see the umbra swelling into enormous shadows as Juno's blood welled across the floor.

"Take the others and go," Zulu said. "I'll take the green car when I've finished with the girl."

The mulatto nodded and disappeared, and Zulu advanced on Echo. She snatched the sacrificial knife from Juno's hand and swiped distantly at Zulu. And the room went dark, all daylight absorbed by the umbra.

Echo dropped to her knees and crawled away. There was a crash, and she heard the dresser mirror shatter, heard Zulu yelp. When she rose to her feet and turned, she could see again. Zulu was swatting at what looked like an electric spider web trying feebly to draw him into the cracked mirror. The lightning threads had encased his head, but seemed unable to do more than distract him. Hoping that would prove enough, Echo leapt forward with the knife and slashed at the vague outline of his chest. The knife blade glanced off the metal bra. Feeling the blow, Zulu caught her wrist and flung her, face-first, into the bedpost.

Echo sank to the floor, barely conscious, sounds of destruction all around her. She thought Zulu's men must be smashing the house to pieces, and she could feel the blood dripping down her face, Juno's blood and her own. Zulu grabbed her by her hair, flung her face-down on the bed. She heard his shrieking laugh, the same laugh she'd heard that night on the pier when the slavers murdered Maggie. She wondered vaguely if the transvestite were likely to rape her before he killed her, hoped that wasn't allowed by the transvestite code or whatever. Then she heard what sounded like clothing dropping to the floor behind her.

She drew back into her special place, the world of sounds, where things were only qualities and patterns of air and she could make them mean whatever she wanted. She thought-felt the diamond flashes of the breaking glasses, the retreating feet drumming on the rich walnut of the stairs. Cars roared to life outside and, beneath that sound, glass splintered and a gun barked, major syncopation. Zulu fell upon her back, and there was a sharp pain in her buttocks—and she thought she must be dead. There was no movement, no sound.

And then Zulu's weight was gone from her back, and a hand rolled her over. The room had lightened to dusk gray. Max stood there holding the Glock, looking uncertain. Echo stared back at him. "Hey," he said finally.

"Hey," she repeated.

Max went over to the window and peeked out like a spy expecting a fusillade of bullets. Car doors slammed and tires screeched. "Pull that dress down for a change and let's get out of here," he said. "You have a nasty cut on your butt, but we don't have time to play doctor."

Echo saw what had made the nasty cut, and her face turned almost as white as her hair. Zulu was lying naked on the floor, blood seeping from a major exit wound in his chest. His dick had been cut off and replaced with six inches of sharpened metal.

"A previous encounter with Z," Max told her. "He caught Zulu trying to collect hair samples and fingernail clippings so he could witch him. Z took his own version of a sample from Zulu. Hard to believe they'd ever work together after that."

Max peered out the window again. "Last night while we were singing, Zulu took out his boss, Jinx, and Z took out Madame Herod. I don't know how he got past her security; it was warded. You know, magicked and charmed and all that shit."

"Charm," Echo echoed. *That's* why Z had her steal Greta's amulet.

"Yeah, maybe he used his charm," Max said. He took her by the elbow and led the stunned girl to the door. The house appeared empty, and they started down the stairs. "Anyway, the son of a bitch is taking over the whole territory, although it looks like he'll have to do it without a witch. Zulu's dead, Juno's dead, and the third one, Greta, is in the trunk of the Jaguar. Some of her is, anyway. I recognized the head." He paused at the front door and looked back at her. "The way I figure it, Z wanted the slave trade for himself, but had to sacrifice Juno because she'd given Greta her word, or charm, or whatever. Hey, you doing okay?"

"Okay."

"I found out the green Jag belonged to Madame Herod, which got me to pop the trunk, which got me to get the hell away from the car just before Zulu arrived with the troops. I vote we find some other means of transportation, by the way." He tucked the gun into the back of his pants, the way they did on TV. "Shit, that pinches." He pulled it back out and cleaned it on his t-shirt and tossed it on the floor. "Shall we get out of here?"

"We?" Echo looked up at him hopefully.

Max grimaced. "We'll talk about that later. Right now, if there's any place you've ever wanted to go, speak up. Z sent us over here, right in Zulu's path, expecting both of us to disappear tonight. I say we oblige him. What do you think? Vegas? San Francisco? Los Angeles?"

"Los," Echo replied softly. She was watching one of the umbra that had followed her partway down the stairs. Now it began gliding back up in the shadow of the balcony. She started crying again. Max gave her a squeeze, then took her hand and led her out into the gathering twilight.

Part II

Los Angeles

7

Maybe I never had a soul.
All I know
is when they put me in the worming hole
I'm gone.
You might as well go fishing in the air
as look for me down there.
                                                    —Max

"A camel has a better chance of fitting through the eye of a needle," Terry the Snake told Max, holding up a cigarette and a hypodermic, "than a rich man has of getting through Needle Park at night."

Max gave him ten bucks, pocketed the needle and lit the Camel. He took a drag and then placed it between Terry's lips. The blind man took a long drag, stuffed the bill in a back pocket, and smiled. Somehow he knew a ten when he felt it, Max thought. "You do talk shit."

"Righteous shit," Terry corrected. A smile cracked his gray-bearded face, wrinkled and brown as old bark. He exhaled the smoke and settled back on the upside-down garbage can that served as his throne.

"Righteous shit," Max agreed. It had not been a real edge-of-your-seat morning in Echo Park, but he had watched a half dozen locals approach Terry the Snake with their offerings, everything from coffee and day-old donuts to cash to the needle Max had just purchased. In return, they got their questions answered. People seemed to trust Terry's take on anything and everything, so Max had decided it couldn't hurt to make himself a client. Now, sitting on the filthy stoop of his apartment building, he had only to figure out what to ask.

"You seem like a pretty knowledgeable guy," he started.

"You gonna ask me about the black stain on your floor."

Max didn't think it was a question. "Yeah. It's kind of spooky. At first I thought it was a burn, but the wood's not charred. Then I thought it was painted on, but it doesn't seem to be coated. It's kind of like a shadow of a person, a body, I mean, but it's like it's the wood itself."

"That's the mark of the new god," Terry told him. "They're all over the place. Sometimes two together."

"What do they mean, exactly?"

"Exactly? They mean somebody died there. Maybe they OD'd, maybe something else. But that black spot on the floor is all that's left of them now."

"Shit." Max reflected. "What do you mean, maybe they died of something else? If it's dangerous, I should get Echo out of here."

"Soul stain."

"What?"

"Whatever took those people took everything physical, but it couldn't take their life force."

"So the black stain is this force?"

Terry shook his head. "That black stain is the mark the life force makes when the body goes and it can't follow."

"Well, I don't follow either. Where does the body go that the spirit-thing can't follow? Into another dimension?"

"The 'spirit-thing' is already in another dimension. That's why your sorry-ass eyes can't see it."

"Like ghosts and shit."

Terry sighed. "Let me put it this way. The new god around here, the one everybody is talking about, is a god of the body. If I tell you he expels the souls, and they make that stain on the floor, you're gonna think I'm crazy."

"Well, I might ask around," Max shrugged. He didn't

know what else to say.

"So, what you doing here, white boy?"

"Seemed like as good a place as any to be lost in." Max didn't want to explain that he and Echo had moved to Echo Park on either a whim or a misunderstanding—not to mention it was right off 101 when the car they'd stolen from Z broke down. The freeway exit sign had mentioned something about Dodger Stadium, but nothing about a room in a ghetto project, a single long room that looked like a closet that looked like a place nightmares escaped from; a dingy room whose ceiling was criss-crossed with exposed pipes from which Echo and Max hung their clothes. (Echo said she thought of the hanging clothes as room dividers, which made the place seem bigger; but they reminded Max of scarecrows warning him away from the only space there was to occupy.) And then there was the black stain.

"But she's black and you're blond," Terry observed, and Max doubted that someone had told Terry that. He probably knew from the way they talked, or smelled, or from the sound of their walks. Max wanted to ask him about that stuff, but before he could, Terry added, "You a West Hollywood couple. How'd you wind up in this particular no-place-special?"

Max shrugged to himself. "We got to LA, saw the sign for Echo Park, and I asked her, 'What do you think, Echo?' She said, 'Echo.' So here we are."

Terry smiled. In some strange sense, Echo Park seemed to be his, not to own or rule over, as Z had the Warehouse District, but to preside over—insofar as a blind, impotent god *can* preside.

"I think she's in shock or something," Max said. He supposed watching someone kill your best friend with a spear and try to rape you with a razor-dick qualified as shocking.

"Or something," Terry mused, pushing his watch cap back on his fuzzy gray-brown hair. "But I asked about you." The eyes were blind, they looked like raw eggs with broken yolks, but the smile was piercing.

Max lit himself a clove. "We had to move in a hurry, had to borrow money, a car . . . Don't know anyone around here." If I need a job, Max thought, I could try for my own *Real Life* show on MTV. "We're kind of used to places like this, though." *This* meaning the off-kilter eight-floor apartment buildings leaning together like dog turds on bare earth. *This* meaning the tattered wino-trees leaning against each other across the street in Echo Park, trees that bore strange fruit: large inhabited cardboard boxes, like giant seed pods. *This* meaning Echo Park itself, where bums without boxes grazed in lost-thought stupor, barely concerned with keeping out of the mud and shit. Max wondered why they didn't put up signs there saying, "Keep Off the Shit."

"Not *we*," Terry said. "You. What are *you* doing here?"

"Oh." Terry had a point. Max *hadn't* come here because of Echo. And Max, being Max, had no inclination to pretend that he was in love with her. "Well, I need to be someplace people won't ask a lot of questions. And *I'm* kind of used to places like this."

"You're kind of used to thinkin' of yourself in this context," Terry corrected. "This context being all anybody remembers of some particular hell." His left hand with his twisted wooden cane, and his right with half a lit cigarette swept out to embrace the burned and rusted cars, the derelicts sleeping in puddles of offal where sidewalk met graffiti-tattooed building, the reef of broken and rusted hypodermics in the gutter along the street. "You *like* to think of yourself in this context, white boy."

"Name's Max."

"I know," chuckled Terry. "You ain't no white boy, either, not really. That's what I'm gettin' at. What gods are in your bodies I do not know, but I know the gods when I meet 'em."

"That's me," Max said, "god of gash, merchant of trash, master of the crash."

"You a musician?" Terry asked.

"Sometimes. Echo is. She's got work already, singing back-up at Capitol. I bet she'll get work with this band that's looking for a girl singer, too. They'd be crazy not to take her."

"You bring your guitar down here sometime and I'll play you your future. Assuming you decide I'm not crazy. Assuming you want to know."

"I think you've got a customer," Max told him. A wizened black woman carrying an infant that couldn't have been her own had stopped a dozen feet away and was staring at them, staring at Terry with some kind of reverence, at Max with impatience.

"Yeah," Terry said, stubbing out his cigarette. Raising his voice, he called out, "Who comes to talk to the Snake?"

"Terry see us?" the lady asked, stepping forward. It's what the others had said too, the others who came to talk to the man: *Terry see us?* An odd invocation to a blind man.

"That you Mrs. Robinson?" Terry asked in a tone that said he knew it was. "And one of your granddaughters. Is that little Amy's child?" Maybe Terry could tell who she was by the smell of her particular shit. Certainly his scrambled eyes never moved, although when Max closed his own eyes he had the faint impression that he could still see Terry's, only swirling like galaxies.

Mrs. Robinson gave Terry a torn envelope, which he slipped into an inner pocket of his frayed brown overcoat. She was asking him about the baby's future. Something about the baby reminded Max of a paper lantern, fragile skin stretched so tight over a white-hot flame you couldn't believe it didn't catch fire and incinerate itself.

"I already put her on the list for St. Agnes pre-school," Mrs. Robinson was saying.

"Get real." Terry's retort was a slap in the face. "This here's a crack baby. You don't need me to tell you she's got no future. You turn her over to Public Health and put your energies into some of those other kids. I told you before, that Alanso Junior gonna be a badass motherfucker like his father if you don't get on his case from the time he starts walking."

"He took his first steps this week," Mrs. Robinson remembered, slightly alarmed. "He got my purse off the kitchen table."

"You don't have enough toes and fingers to plug every crack in the dike," Terry scolded her. "You do what I say, or the flood gonna sweep you away."

The old black lady gave the infant in her arms a look that broke Max's heart. He could see that she loved the damaged life.

"What you lookin' at?" she spat at Max, who was too surprised to respond.

"He's my anti-social worker," Terry said. "Don't mind his pitiful ass."

"Social worker." She crossed herself with her free hand, or maybe it was the sign of the pentagram she made, or some other gesture. "I was wonderin' what a white boy was doin' here." And with this new anger to distract her from her grief, she was able to get herself moving back up the street.

Max watched her go. "You want a clove?" he finally asked Terry.

"A clove? I can understand people smokin' crack, but cloves? Why don't you just roll a little shit in a ZigZag and smoke that?"

Max grinned, then thought of Z and frowned.

"Ain't nobody comin' after you," Terry informed him. "You just chasin' yourself."

"How do you know?" Max asked, lighting a clove for himself.

"It's my nature to know. Like I know the worst thing that can happen to you, is that you'll catch up to yourself."

Max took the needle from his pocket, held the tip up to the sun and tried to stare at it. He thought of someone trying to pierce the yolk of Terry's eye with a needle or a knife point, and the eye suddenly exploding outward with an inner light, with a nuclear energy that fried everything around it, that reduced Echo Park—or Needle Park, as the locals called it—to carbon shadows on blast-whitened walls. A park was supposed to be . . . what? The parks around his parents' home had been mythic paradox, artificially blessed pristine greenery, Disneyesque. Parks were fairytale places, like Grimm's forests; but urban fairytales weren't pretty these days. Max looked across the street, at a guy nodding on a park bench, at a couple of young gay hustlers, at three black teenagers in gang colors and baggies, their arms outstretched like crosses on a hill.

Max was thinking about crossing the street when the police car came around the corner. It was a gray Taurus, unmarked, but it didn't take Max's years of street experience to pick up on it. It was too conspicuously bland to be a person's car. "Cops, coming this way," he told Terry.

Terry grunted, not even raising his blind eyes from the pavement.

There were two men in the car, a big, mean-looking middle-aged black man who stayed behind the wheel, and a white guy in his mid-twenties, who got out as the car coasted up in front of them. He was a hair over six feet, lean and tough-looking, but with a handsome face under his mop of black hair. He came around the front of the car, and as he walked right up to the man on the ash can, he said, "Terry see us?"

Now Terry raised his scrambled egg eyes and there was an expression, not the half-playful querulousness Max had seen earlier, but real anger. "I don't see you now. I don't see you ever again."

The cop sighed, looked briefly at Max, then looked at him again in a slightly startled way. He said to Terry, "Look, I know you hate us, that you think you have reason to hate us. I didn't come here to argue about your reasons. But we had another of those murders last night, and can't get shit on it."

"Maybe it was a suicide," Terry suggested.

"Right. Nearly twenty people, mostly unconnected to each other, all decide to commit suicide by overdosing on E^2 so bad it melts them right into the concrete. We can't even get a sample of this mystery drug. Looks like murder to me."

"So you want me to argue with your reasons?" There was still anger in his voice.

"I want you to tell me something. Anything. You know every goddamn thing that goes down in Echo Park."

Terry didn't respond.

The cop snuck another glance at Max, who returned his best blank-confused-apologetic stare, the one he always used with cops. "Terry, you care about these people. I know you do. I hear about you helping, or trying to help the folks down here all the time. Help me stop this killing."

"Like you stopped it last time?"

"Terry, you know I wasn't even a cop then."

"But you bring that motherfucking bastard Nemo down here with you."

The young cop moved a little closer, spoke a little more

quietly. "He's my partner. He's senior. I have no say about that."

"And I got nothing to say to you."

The young cop raised his hands to the sky, shot Max another look, and went back to his car.

"Interesting," Max said, as the Taurus disappeared around a corner. He'd expected to be rousted when Terry didn't produce.

"That was Michael. Not a bad boy, but he ain't the Archangel he thinks he is."

"And that other guy? Nemo?"

"Another story altogether." Terry spat on the pavement and said no more.

8

You strive to be misunderstood
With your artificial artificiality.
                    —Max

Like a wet fire, Echo was all hope and fear. She'd slept half the drive across the country, missing Texas and New Mexico entirely, which Max said was a good thing unless you liked flat, brown, and ugly, no offense to her, since she wasn't ugly. Ha-ha, she'd thought, but she couldn't say it.

Was she really cursed? It wasn't like a hand grabbed her throat when she tried to talk. She just couldn't bring herself to do it, like the words were sleeping babies she didn't want to wake up, was afraid to wake up, lest she see in their opening eyes something awful, like in that Terry man's.

When they'd discovered snow in Flagstaff, Arizona, it was as if Max were her Tibetan guide, sharing this sacred material for the first time with the Southern girl who'd never touched a flake. Max started singing perverted Christmas carols until, unthinkingly, she joined in, and she was so glad she could still sing she started crying, crying and smiling and singing all at the same time, until Max was choking with laughter.

And then she'd slept again, and when Max woke her late that night they were in LA, where the freeway was no longer lined with trees or snow or desert but with a million burnished stars, each with its own solar system of human lives, chaotic or cruel, grandiose or crippled.

The gods, of course, enjoy cruel jokes, especially when they're played on the same entities who, ultimately, can't retaliate, who might temporarily lay waste to a god's favorite land, as a dog might shit on a Persian carpet. Echo Park was a shithole worse even than some of the flops Echo had been forced to share in New Orleans. Drugs and crime were Column A and Column B on the daily menu. The park was surrounded by projects inhabited not by humans so much as reverberations of humans, lost people who were noise out of context, who bounced aimlessly from one denser object to another, diminished at every contact.

When they'd wandered into the project where they now lived, they'd simply found an empty apartment that wasn't too filthy and flopped there for the night. Echo could tell Max wished he still had the Glock. But they'd piled all their stuff against the door, and in the morning, when a wicked looking black man pushed his way in anyway, claiming he was the landlord (well, in a way), he'd simply taken the money Max offered him and left them alone after a few lewd inquiries about Echo's pussy, like it was a car he was considering purchasing. She'd noticed the way he pretended not to see the big black stain on the floor near their blanket, so maybe he was a landlord after all, the kind who didn't like cleaning up anything.

It was her fear and loathing of the place that got her to drag Max out of bed the first day, when she would rather have forced him to stay there, forced him to make love to her properly, as he had refused to do all the way across the country.

Max had taken her over to Capitol Records. They'd both ogled the big, round, stacked building from the freeway the night before, so it seemed like a good place to start, and after charming their way past a couple of secretaries, they'd found a cattle call for back-up singers. There didn't seem to be anything for guys, so while Echo waited her turn, Max wandered around hoping to find some trace of Daniel, or maybe one of the R&D people who'd noticed him in New Orleans.

The audition itself was simple enough. Echo had sung for smaller crowds than the one in the sound booth, many times. They played her a little of this, a little of that and had her sing along, which was her forte, of course. Despite their hip glamour and affected grunge, the studio guys reminded her of English gentlemen, showing the fox to the hounds and then smiling pridefully to each other when the stupid beasts actually chased it.

After the audition, Max was waiting there on a bench. He'd picked up an audition card for a girl singer for a new band named NREmission, which he gave to Echo. When she told him she'd been hired, he was genuinely thrilled for her. She went to work that same day, so excited at the prospect of working around recording equipment for the first time, she forgot about being afraid. Max went back to Echo Park.

Echo's part was relatively simple. They started her with some songs that were already laid down, so that she was alone in the sound studio with the other two back-ups, a heavy black woman named Shirley who could have been any age from thirty to fifty, and a white chick named Cash, thin, blond, and obviously in her early twenties. Echo smiled and agreed a lot, and, when they saw how much she put into her little part, that she didn't treat this job as an insignificant stepping stone on the way to inevitable stardom, they liked her. They did a couple of R&B tunes, one by an artist whose voice Echo recognized, and she actually looked around, as if he might be in the room.

By the end of the first day, she was emotionally exhausted. She left the building with Shirley and Cash, handed a cab driver the address she'd written down, and lay down sideways in the back seat, like a little kid, giving her swollen brain a chance to rest while riding back to Echo Park. She had the driver stop at a deli, where she got a couple pre-packaged sandwiches for dinner, overpriced submarines with mystery meat and questionable vegetables. Still, it would do for a celebration until she got paid.

It was dark when she got to the apartment building. After a moment's hesitation, which she could see was freaking out the cab driver, she forced herself out onto the sidewalk and quickly past the half-dazed population lingering on the street and stoop. The creepy old blind man sitting on a garbage can smiled at her, but she rushed past him, and into the building.

This building breathed. A lot of them did, but this one had been breathing out for a long time, trying to expel whatever was in it. Once back in Athens she'd gone on a tour of an old slave quarters with her junior high history class, and what she'd felt in one darkened hut with its packed dirt floor knocked her right to the ground and fell on her. The teacher, a big man, had a hard time getting the seventy pound girl back on her feet. She was screaming about being covered with something like boiling dough. Couldn't stop crying for a week.

Echo could not have explained it to Max any more than she'd been able to explain it to her high school teacher, but a home is not just a building; it exists in many dimensions. And this diseased, necrotic apartment building was equally bad off in all of them. It had stopped trying to hide its creeping infection. This building wheezed.

Holding her breath, feeling like she was slogging through an open wound, Echo climbed the four flights to their apartment. There would be light inside, the light of Max's beauty, and she would tell him how great the studio was, tell him in real words, her own words, break the curse then and there. She pushed at the door and found it open.

Inside, Max lay sprawled on the blanket they were using for a bed. His body was practically a mirror image of the black stain on the floor next to him. No, he wasn't dead. She knew that. She'd seen junkies nodded out before, her sister for one. But seeing Max in this condition shocked her, backed her up, right out the still-open door and onto the landing, and she took no notice of the boys coming up behind her, though they weren't being particularly quiet. One moment she was pressing the sandwich bag she'd brought home in both hands in front of her, and the next she had been grabbed at the elbows by two boys, young men actually, who dragged her back down the stairs, her heels going bump-bump-bump on the steps. They seemed in no particular hurry, didn't say anything nasty to her; in fact they were talking about something else altogether, a party, it sounded like, and drugs, and some other girls. Maybe they were talking about the girl Echo saw when she looked back up the stairs, the girl following along about a half-flight behind. Echo tried to scream to her for help, but nothing came out. The girl just smiled reassuringly and followed along. Bump, bump, bump.

As they emerged from the building, the night exploded around Echo, racket coming from the park across the street, a steel band, the shouts of revelers. A handful of people were chanting something, some unfamiliar name that she couldn't quite make out. The men scattered around the front stoop were looking in the direction of the park, and didn't seem to notice Echo being kidnaped until a gruff voice said, "Whoa!"

It was the creepy blind man on the garbage can, Terry. He was holding out his cane, blocking their path. "Where you boys going with that girl?" he asked in a friendly but inquisitorial tone, the tone a grandparent might use with a child.

Echo took the opportunity to struggle to her feet and twist out of their grasps. They let her go, but the other girl was now coming down the stoop, blocking Echo's retreat.

"To the party!" one of them howled into the night.

"Bakas!" the other yelled.

"Yeah, well, you ain't takin' her, 'cause she's bringin' me my dinner. Now get along."

The girl pushed past Echo, her smile indifferent now, and the three marched across the street without another word.

Echo couldn't help holding her breath. Even in the near dark of the stoop, the blind man's eyes were horrible, messed up, almost like someone had painted black whorls on an Easter egg shell. She'd seen a guy in New Orleans with cat's eyes, and Juno had told her they were really contact lenses, and she thought, *Maybe that's what this old man has, contact lenses*, because his face was turned right toward her now, and he didn't seem to be missing anything. But contact lenses couldn't explain the faint golden-red glow that had appeared around his head now that the evening had darkened.

"What'd you bring old Terry, Miss Echo? Smells like a submarine sandwich."

"Submarine sandwich," she agreed. She could buy into the guy having a great smeller—her grandmother, blind from birth, had been really good with smelling and hearing—but how the hell did he know her name?

"Max told me all about you," he said, reaching out expectantly for her package.

"Max?" She handed the formerly precious sandwiches over to him.

"He said you have a beautiful voice."

"A beautiful voice." She said it almost despairingly, but Terry appeared not to notice. He was busy rummaging through the sandwich bag.

"I don't need but one of these. Why don't you sit down here and have the other?"

Why not? she thought. Max wasn't getting up to eat anytime soon. Of course, there *was* this business with Terry's aura. It was as if gold could bleed. Had bled. She leaned against the same wrought iron fence Terry's garbage can was set against and unwrapped the remaining sandwich. Across the street, the chants were getting louder. Now she could make out the name, the same one her partynaper had just shouted: Bakas.

Terry paused between mouthfuls, considered the racket. "You ever hear of Bakas before?"

"Bakas?" she asked.

"He's the Thang 'round here, got it goin' on, ya know? You don't talk like that? Good. But you get my meaning."

Echo grunted through her sandwich. She hadn't realized how hungry she was.

"This Bakas," continued Terry, "he's more a legend than a person. No one's seen him, least not so as to identify, detain, and question. But his followers give out this drug at his parties, drug called E^2. Not just ecstasy, something way more powerful. It ain't square, though, it's round with a hole in the middle, 'cause it's eating you when you think you're eating it. Supposed to be the ultimate high. You get high, girl?"

Echo gagged on her sandwich.

"Good answer. What people mean by 'high' is losing a part of themselves, the heavy parts that weigh you down, sandbag you to this dimension. E^2 lets you lose everything. You stay away from that shit, you hear?"

"Hear," she said. There was something about the old guy she couldn't help liking. She'd never known her own grandfather. Like most of the men in her family, he'd either died young or run off; Grandma told it both ways. But Terry was like she imagined a grandfather would be. If your grandfather were an enforcer for the mob.

"This E^2, it turns some people into black spots," Terry added.

Echo choked again, this time for real. What if Max had taken it and—

Terry reassured her before she could finish the thought. "I didn't tell Max about that exactly, 'cause he strikes me as the type who'll have to run right out and try it, but I made him promise not to take anything without checkin' it out with me first. Told him I know all the good shit from the bad around here."

Echo stared at him, suddenly not liking this grandfather so much.

"I can't keep him off the horse, girl. Only he can do that. But if you need my help, I'm stayin' down there." He indicated a door just below street level, behind where they were sitting. There were no windows in the subterranean apartment, Echo noticed. "I stay there, but I dwell where you do. Say, why don't you sing me that song now?"

So Echo sang him "Can't Help Lovin' Dat Man," a capella, low and sad, while they watched the park across the street vomit up revelers, and the one person she really wanted to be with lay unconscious upstairs.

9

All my tracks lead back to you.
When at home, do as the homos do.
                                              —Max

"Terry see us?"

"I hear your ass dustin' my stoop, Max. What you got to tell me?"

It was another smog-dusty simmering day at Echo Park. Max lit a clove. "Nothing."

"You gonna make me do all the work? That, and you still don't have no real smokes?"

"Here." Max pulled a second pack, Camels, from his pocket and lit one for Terry. "Well, Echo's doing great at the studio. She can sing anything, never gives them any trouble."

"Because she don't want to or because she can't?"

"Well, I don't think she wants to. She's just happy to get paid for singing."

"Of course, since she don't talk, and you probably don't make a lot of inquiries, how would you know?"

Max sighed.

Terry reached over and plucked deftly at Max's wardrobe. "Notice you've taken to wearing long-sleeve shirts in the heat. You been out applying for jobs?"

"Not really," Max admitted with one of his winning grins.

Being blind, Terry was unimpressed. "How long you gonna let that girl support your sad ass while you shoot dope?"

"Lots of guys around here don't have jobs."

Terry nodded. "Right. They let their old ladies support them. But you and I know Echo ain't your old lady. At least, that's what you think."

"You're right. I'm taking advantage of her. I'm disgusting." He even said it with conviction. "Know any good pimps?"

"You *are* disgusting. Shoot smack. Open your crack. That's a career option for some people. It's an insult to the gods when *you* do it. And mark my word, boy, you're gonna pay."

Max was silent until he'd finished his clove and stubbed it out on the step; he was probably the only one in a three-mile radius who actually collected his own butts and threw them out. "How do I pay for not knowing what the hell to do with my life? I thought wasting it *was* the ultimate penalty."

Terry shook his head. "You can't play Br'er Rabbit with the gods, tellin' 'em, 'Oh, please, don't let me be a junky whore and waste all my talent,' when that's exactly what you want to do. No, no. Payment's gonna hurt, little white motherfuckin' brother."

"So, you think there's some philosophical reason it matters what the hell I do with my life?"

"Hell yeah, it matters. It matters to you, and you just ain't admitting it. You figure, Love is the only thing that's important, and anything I might do—play music, be a decent boyfriend or husband—would only be important to prove I'm worthy of love, and I can't ever do that, because I'm *already* loved by everybody. Every friggin' person I meet falls in love with me. So being loved means nothing to me. Don't that about sum it up?"

"Shit."

"So what *is* your philosophy?"

"In the beginning," said Max, "is all this lumpy shit called the universe. You're born, and you try to make something out of the lumpy shit, but even if you somehow do make something, in the back of your mind you know it's just lumpy shit.

"So tell me, Terry, is God your copilot, or what?"

"God used to be my copilot. But we crashed into a mountain, and I had to eat Him."

Max laughed. "But what's love got to do with it?"

"You know the myth of Sisyphus?"

Max thought for a moment. "Not a bad name for a CD."

"Sisyphus was a greedy king, never satisfied. Always had to have more than whatever he had. The gods sentenced him to the eternal torment of rolling a big boulder almost all the way up a hill, only to have it slip past him at the last second and roll back down again. So one day he's out rolling the rock, and he thinks maybe he's got it this time. He *always* thinks maybe he's got it this time, that's part of the torture, but this time, just as he thinks he's about got that big rock to the top, he sees out of the corner of his eye somebody coming up over the top of the hill from the other side, and he loses it. Falls flat on his face. Rock thunders back down the hill. When he looks up, he sees this dusty, dirty little Jew in a long black coat and buttoned up shoes and one of those big flat hats, like the jewelry guys over on Rodeo Drive wear. Got a long scraggy gray beard and sideburns like ZZ Top. And the guy is just staring at him with an amused expression.

"Sisyphus starts to get up, and by the time he's on his knees, he's already as tall as the Jew. He's been pushing this rock forever, and he's a big strong motherfucker."

"Like Conan with that mill wheel," Max suggested.

"Right. Chin like the prow of a boat and teeth to scare the sharks. Got the Conan outfit on, too. So he says to the Jew, 'You lookin' at me?'"

"That's not Conan, that's Robert DeNiro."

"Shut up, smart ass. We're talkin' about Sisyphus. The Jew says, 'Well, I was just wondering why you were rolling that rock up this hill. There's no room for it up here.'

"'I have to,' Sisyphus says. 'I'm Sisyphus.'

"'Oh,' the Jew says. 'I think I heard of you. You gonna lie on that rock and let the vultures peck out your liver or something?'

"'No,' Sisyphus says, 'that's somebody else.' Sisyphus gets all the way to his feet so he towers over the Jew. 'I just roll the rock. I get it almost all the way up, and then it rolls back down again. Rock and roll. That's it.'

"'Why?'

"Sisyphus looks away and mumbles something, but the Jew keeps pestering him until he says, 'I was greedy. I always wanted more, for no particular reason except to have more.'

"The Jew nods slowly. 'I get it. So you have to keep working forever at this meaningless task. Ha. You got it easy.'

"Sisyphus looks down on him with this glower that causes all the grass on the top of the hill to start smokin', and asks him what the fuck he means by that. 'Well,' says the Jew, 'I'm the Wandering Jew. Maybe you heard of me? I was in Jerusalem one day when I see this naked guy carrying a cross down the street, leading a big parade. People are wailing, there's a protest, the whole schmeer. I'm late for a bris, so I tell the guy, 'Hey, can you hurry up with that cross? Some of us have jobs to get to, families to feed.' And he looks at me and says, 'My journey will be over soon, but you will wander the earth until I return again.' Yeesh. How was I supposed to know it was the Son of God?'"

"Bummer," Max offered.

"Sisyphus wasn't so sympathetic," Terry continued. "He says, 'So big deal, at least you get a change of scenery. I'm stuck with a rock. My crime was only against myself, and I know that now, so all this rock and rolling is useless. But you, you're being punished for a reason. And then there's an end in sight, too, when that Son of God fella comes back.'

"'Hmmm,' the Jew says again. 'Well, I think you got it

easy because you can accept the fact your punishment is deserved. You can take pride, even, in just rolling the rock and not pissing and moaning. Me, I have all this guilt.'

"Sisyphus looks at the little Jew for a minute. Then he says, 'You wanna switch?'"

Max waited for him to go on, but he didn't. "Terry?"

"You wanna switch?" Terry asked quietly.

Max wandered over to the park, stepping over the needles and glycine packets and fast-food wrappers, this archeology of extinction, into the alternative past, where men lived in boxes, where skeletonized appliances rested on rusted lawn furniture like sleeping suburban robots. He rapped on a familiar box promising a heavy-duty Kenmore washer. It was a minor mistake, because it had rained that morning and his rapping dislodged some loose water, eliciting fierce cursing from within and a sudden eruption of rags and newspapers right through the jack-in-the-box top. The newspapers flew everywhere, but the rags stayed more or less together. "Hey, Jack," Max said apologetically. "Ready to score?"

The nightmare whirling of scarecrow parts stopped, shook itself briefly like a dog, revealing a small man of indeterminate color and age. Max called him Jack, but others called him Jocko or Johnny, or Juan, or Itch. "Whatthemuthafuckinhey-awrightokay," he said. Then he disappeared briefly down into the box, came out again with his pockets bulging and two rocks in each hand. While Max scanned one of the newspapers, a free weekly devoted to the singles scene for people who liked to wear dog collars, Itch collapsed the box, and laid a stone at each corner. Then they set off across the park together.

"You interested in dating from the personals?" Max started casually, knowing the man was probably illiterate and chose his insulation for its R value rather than its reading value.

Juan looked at him as if he were insane.

"Hey, Jack, what about this E^2 stuff?"

"Praise Bakas," Itch said without looking up from the ground. He seemed to know the entire park, not by the trees or walkways or visible streets, but by the minute signatures of the grass and even the dirt itself. He was a bloodhound, sniffing with his eyes.

"Say what?" asked Max, refining his laugh to a trace element.

"Praise Bakas," Jack repeated, still without looking up or slowing down. "You have to say that every time someone mentions E^2 or you could get fucked. Say it."

"What?"

"Praise Bakas. I said E^2, so you have to say it."

"Praise Bakas," Max replied. "Now can I have some?"

"No. I can get you smack, but not E^2. Say it."

"Praise Bakas," Max complied. "Why not?"

"Nobody sells it. They just give it away. At the raves, the *Bakanas*."

"Nobody gives away shit," Max said. "That's in both the Ten Commandments and the Bill of Rights."

"We're going to get smack, right?" Jocko asked.

"We could get both," Max said. "What do you take with it, anyway?"

"Your chances," Johnny said. "How much you got?"

When they cleared the Park, Itch took them past a crack house down to a Denny's, where Max bought coffee for the two of them. Itch headed for the bathroom for a badly needed morning shit and general cleansing. Not to mention the score. This particular Denny's was such a well known drug drop that its patrons called it Bennies. Whoever was selling that day would follow Itch into the men's room and go into the next stall. Itch would pass the cash Max had given him through a peep-hole in the metal divider and receive the smack back the same way in a small glycine envelope. Rip-offs were rarer than might be imagined, and Max only had to watch the restaurant entrance to make sure Itch didn't forget for whom he'd made the purchase.

Except this time Itch didn't come back alone.

It was the two cops who'd stopped to talk to Terry. The big black one was dragging Itch, but holding him at arm's length, far enough away to not get any of the vagrant's outer crust on himself. Max looked down at his coffee, hoping they'd pass right by and keep walking out the door, that Itch hadn't fingered him, because, hey, weren't junkies the most honorable, reliable, standup guys on Earth?

The parade stopped at his booth. Nemo had in his hand the bills Max had given Itch. He stuffed them into Max's half-full cup.

Max looked up with a faint smile. "Thanks, but I've already got this round."

The big black man raised a fist about four feet over Max's head, and Max had a brief flashback to a rock avalanche somewhere, a boulder tumbling down a mountain right at his head. And then . . . and then the other cop stepped in and locked up Nemo's arm before it could descend. "That's not the idea, remember?" he told his partner.

"He'll never talk," Nemo grumbled. "And when he don't, I'm using his skin to send that blind nigger a braille message."

"Go outside and play with the junkie," the younger cop suggested in a pleasant, almost cajoling voice. The big man made a noise, reached into Max's cup for the paper money, squeezed it out over the table, and headed toward the door with his catch.

"Michael," the young cop said, extending his hand, and

Max shook it. The grip was warm and electric, as Max had expected it would be.

"Max."

Michael sat down on the bench opposite Max and pulled over the cup that had been intended for Itch. "That was my partner, Nemo."

"Perfect. He *looks* like something from 20,000 leagues under the sea. Moves kind of like a whale. A whale as it rolls to eye your fishing trawler, then crushes it with its tail."

"He thinks you're involved with Bakas, and that you and Terry are in league to make the police look bad. Of course, he also firmly believes Humpty Dumpty was pushed." He grinned, then gestured for a waitress.

"What do you believe, Michael?"

The waitress came over and stared blankly at Max's half-filled cup and the mess on the table. Finally Michael asked if they could have another cup and a rag, and she shuffled off, probably to tell the cook about such a strange and wondrous request. The two men sat looking at each other, like figures in a Hopper painting, until she returned with a fresh cup of coffee and made a brief swipe at the Formica table top with a dish rag.

Michael said, "I believe you're a runaway. I think you've been on the street for a while. I think you ran here from new trouble someplace where you didn't get much sun. You have ID?"

"No."

"Ever been pulled over on a traffic stop?"

"Don't drive."

"How do you get into the places you . . . want to get into?"

"I smile." Max smiled his please-let-me-in smile. "They either let me in or they don't."

"How do you make a living?"

"We're musicians. My friend is a singer. She's got studio work right now. I'm still looking." He sipped his coffee thoughtfully.

"You're wearing long sleeves. You weren't, the first day I saw you."

"Like you said, I'm not used to being outside during the day much. Don't want to get skin cancer."

Now it was Michael's turn to sip and stare thoughtfully. "Most beginners shoot between their toes, so it won't be visible. But you *want* people to know." When there was no response, he continued: "We were waiting here for you. I wanted to talk to you when Terry wasn't around."

To have some leverage, Max thought. "What's your problem with Terry?"

"It's more like his problem with us. Nobody told you how he was blinded?"

Max shook his head.

"Before he became . . . what he is now, Terry was a neighborhood organizer. Had the respect of everybody around Echo Park, and even had some success establishing drug-free zones down here by playing the gangs off against each other. Which, in the end, was a problem. Neither gang *wanted* to respect what Terry was doing, but each was afraid that if it did him, the locals would get behind the other gang. So Terry walked that tight rope for a couple years, always pushing for a little bit more and usually getting it, but in the end his own success undid him."

"'Undid him'?" Max snorted.

Michael grimaced but went on. "There was a turf dispute between the Bloods and the Crips, and they decided to have Terry arbitrate."

"Shit." Max wasn't laughing now.

"He was fucked. If he refused, he lost the community's respect. If he decided in favor of one gang, the other was going to be real unhappy. So Terry took what he hoped would be a way out, and would help the community besides. He declared the turf another free zone."

"Which didn't please either side."

"You been around gangs before?"

Max shrugged.

"Somebody decided only a blind man couldn't have seen it their way." He took a swallow of his coffee, and looked out the window. Max looked too, saw the same nothing. "They fucked him up so bad there was nothing to reconstruct. The Mayor sent his personal physician, the community took up a collection, etcetera. We wanted him to talk, of course. We had him locked up tight, and we wanted to take a crack at one of those gangs, when they couldn't just take out the witness.

"Terry had a wife and kids, did I tell you that?" Michael and Max locked eyes on the next sip. "I wasn't a cop yet. Still in the academy. Nemo was head detective down here. He's from these same streets, thinks the academy and the courts are full of shit. Always takes the straight line between two points, no matter whose head is in the way."

"He tried to play hardball with Terry, and the Snake told him to fuck himself?"

Michael nodded. "Terry has quite a reputation as a fortune teller *these* days, but . . . And Nemo, he just didn't think it out. He figured he could flush out whoever had done it to Terry by putting out the word that Terry had talked. Not smart really. They didn't have to come after Terry. The kids, the wife, very ugly. Terry still didn't talk, because now he had a new enemy."

"Nemo. Excuse me, but your partner's a dick."

"He's who he is, a good cop in his way. The only way he knows."

"So he's a hard dick. How can he imagine Terry would *ever* talk to you guys?"

"Nemo just can't admit he made a mistake, can't accept the blame for the wife and kids."

"He tell you that, or are you just overanalyzing a pit bull?"

"Shit. Look, let's talk about you and this Bakas thing. My thinking on this is that Terry wants to help protect the people in his old 'hood from Bakas, but he can't because of this thing with Nemo."

"Maybe with cops."

"Maybe. But if you were to inquire discreetly from Terry and then just as discreetly let us know what you heard, we might be able to stop a lot of people from being killed, and the mayor from declaring a public emergency and bringing the national guard in here to clean all the undesirables out of Echo Park."

"You mean, runaways without ID?"

Michael shrugged. "These are the facts. Will you help?"

"What am I supposed to find out?"

"You've seen the graffiti, $E^2 = MC$, Bakas Rules? Stuff like that? You must have, it's everywhere. You've seen the black bodies. I know there's one in your room."

"You've been in my room?"

"Not officially. I had to prove to Nemo you weren't part of this Bakas thing before he'd agree to this. He wanted to run your ass in to teach Terry a lesson."

"He's a slow learner."

"Just talk to Terry and let me know, okay?"

Max thought about the weird shit Terry had tried to explain to him the first day, about how the souls that couldn't follow the bodies made the black marks. He decided to keep his mouth shut about that part. "Okay."

Michael and Max looked across the table for a moment. Both their cups were empty. They smiled at the same time, and Michael said, "Don't you want to ask me for fake ID or money or something?"

"Got a match?" Max asked, pulling out a clove.

"You can't smoke in here."

Max got up to leave, but Michael grabbed his arm as he passed by the table. He reached up with his lighter and flared it open.

Max lit his clove and then, as Michael closed the lighter, he bent down and kissed the cop on the cheek.

Michael let go of his arm. "You ever been fingerprinted?"

"Nope." Well, he had been once, but he thought Z had taken care of that.

Michael apparently caught the hesitation. "We'll see." He picked up Max's empty coffee cup.

10

I am a hurricane dressed in bodies.
—Max

Echo didn't like having a park named after her, not this park. She'd been thinking more along the lines of her personal Garden of Eden, but so far Max was a reluctant Adam and Terry the Snake only told her things she didn't want to hear. Not that she doubted the words. She could hear the black hole at the center of the blind man sucking in everything around him, not the things themselves, of course, but their meanings, the ghosts of their souls. She doubted he could have lied if he'd wanted to, because he was so full of truth. But he never said, "Hey girl, you're gonna cut a great groove today." He never said, "This is what you need to do to make Max love you."

The park sucked. Back home, parks had been places for kids to play. In Athens, when she'd taken her sister's little girl to the park, she could feel the confluence of the trees and grass, the squirrels and birds, wrapping the tiny soul in their vibes, teaching her what Mother Earth felt like, the way Echo tried to teach her what a mother felt like in the absence of Echo's junkie sister. This park, Echo Park, had an otherworldly feel too, but it was a world that belonged beneath the roots, beneath the mud. It was the mouth of a place she didn't want to go. She wasn't surprised the buildings seemed to lean toward it. They were being sucked in.

And so was Max. That was the painful part. The park dwellers were empty shells, light as a feather, no ability to resist. But Max was so full of life that he had to *want* it to suck him in. She didn't know how much time she had, or how to use it.

The good part of her life was work. Capitol used her almost every day, and she'd been offered outside gigs by the other girls, although she hadn't taken them because she hadn't given up on Max yet and wanted to be with him, even if it meant wandering the damn park at night, dancing to the boombox music at the *Bakanas*; watching the men and women swirl around him, hoping for a touch; and watching Max spend their money on drugs, money that could have gotten them out this shithole, except she didn't dare not give it to him, because he would have just shrugged and earned his own, turning tricks outside Dodger Stadium, which he called Roger Stadium.

Her third week at Capitol, she had a down day when the rocker she was supposed to sing for was arrested in the early morning hours, and, as Echo had no phone, no one was able to call her off. When she arrived at the studio, there was a message from Cash, who said she'd sung back-up for a band the night before, the same NREmission Max had told her about on her first day. Cash said the band wanted to hear her.

Which turned out to be not exactly true, since it wasn't the whole band, but just one member. When she got to Chez Blues, the little club on Sunset, Daniel was waiting for her behind his drums. "Echo! Echo!" When she didn't respond, he said, "Sorry, I bet you get that a lot."

She gave him a smirk and a hug, and the hands-on-her-hips thing, that meant, Explain your ass, my man.

"Technically I don't run the group," he said, "but I'm the only one who's here and sober every night. How the hell are you?" He gave Echo a huge hug, about a third of which she returned. When her only response was a questioning look, he added. "Right. Oh, don't call me Daniel. I go by Perry now. Want a beer? Coffee?"

"Coffee."

He led her by the hand over to the bar, where he sat her down; then he walked around behind the bar and poured them each a cup of something that had been brewing as long as the La Brea tar pits. He said, "Okay, maybe I'm a little paranoid with the name change, but you didn't work for Z as long as I did. You didn't see some of the stuff he did to people, just because."

Echo thought of Zulu, of what Z had arranged for her. She shuddered and saw, in the bar mirror, Daniel putting his jean jacket over her shoulders.

"Cold in here. Well, at least the coffee's hot. Anyway, Perry will do for the credits, and I plan on keeping my face off of CD covers."

"CD covers?"

Daniel looked relieved to get a response, not to mention a sign of interest. He'd been talking nervously, beads of sweat on his forehead, translucent gems forming a band across his brow. Echo usually thought men in love looked kind of cute, like puppies overly eager to please, but Daniel's over-eager attention had always made her nervous. "Yeah, well, I'm getting ahead of myself, but it looks like we have a contract. We have a final audition coming up in a couple weeks, but that's mostly to decide on material. That's why I wanted to talk to you. To see if you're . . . available."

"Available?"

Daniel blushed. "I mean, if you can do a couple gigs with us, see if you can work in. When you played with us in Orleans, you were sensational. We all loved Max, but—"

"But . . . Max?" Echo frowned at her cooling cup of coffee.

Daniel looked confused. "Is he here with you?"

Echo nodded.

"Shit. Cash didn't say anything about him. He hasn't been

working with you at Capitol?"

Echo shook her head. "Hasn't been working."

Daniel stroked his fuzzy chin. "Well, we've *got* a lead guitar. He should be here now, in fact. I wanted you to get acquainted. I didn't *plan* to just get you here alone, ha ha. But Jet isn't exactly reliable. I should have figured today might be a problem. We got our advance just the other day. Option money, to keep us from signing with anyone else until we finalize the contract. Jet will have it spent by next week when the real money comes in." He frowned. "These guys can be a little rough, but they're damn good. The only reason I got on with them right away is that, well, I'm used to rough. So are you. Anyway, I don't know if there's room for Max."

Echo gave him a pleading look.

"Shit, I guess we could at least see if we can work him in. Can you bring him with you here, nine tonight?"

"Tonight," Echo nodded.

Daniel sat close to her, touched her hand occasionally, talked some more about the band, about the kind of work they were doing, mostly grunge covers. He showed her a play list and gave her a demo tape the band had cut, and she printed out several numbers in her childish scrawl on a paper napkin, adding the place and time and the name of the band, and the initial D. She smiled and nodded to Daniel, and pretty soon she left, smiling and nodding all the way home in the cab, hoping to get there before Max left for the park to score.

As the cab pulled up across from Echo Park, she saw she was in luck. Max was sitting on the stoop talking to Terry and smoking a clove. He gave her a sheepish grin. Terry asked if she was bringing him lunch now as well as dinner. She belted out a couple bars of "There's No Business Like Show Business" and handed Max the napkin.

"D? You found Daniel?" Max asked.

"Daniel," agreed Echo with a big grin.

"This is a play list? You're gonna sing with his band?"

She nodded and then, trying not to show doubt, pointed to Max.

"Me too?" Max looked doubtful. "Tonight? I can't go tonight. I was just telling Terry—"

"If you don't go tonight," Terry interrupted, "I won't tell you who to look for tonight *or* tomorrow."

Max looked startled, said, "Well I can come and watch you, anyway. I mean, I don't have a guitar, I haven't practiced in a month, I . . . " His voice faltered as he looked at her eyes. "I could keep you company. Maybe . . . You want me to come?"

"Come," she begged.

"Okay. But I have to meet . . . someone first. I can meet you over there."

She shook her head, grabbed the crook of his arm, pulled up his unbuttoned sleeve, and pointed at the track marks, submerged trash running down the river of his veins.

"I'll be sober. I promise."

She shook her head again, pleading with her eyes.

"Who you meetin'?" Terry asked for her.

"It's supposed to be a surprise," Max responded vaguely. He wondered if Terry already knew, the way he seemed to know everything. But betrayal by its very nature was always a surprise.

"Surprise?"

"Really," Max protested. "I promise. It's nothing bad. It'll only take a couple hours. You've been up since early and this is a big night. You catch a nap and I'll come back for you. Terry'll watch the door."

"Does this mean no lunch?" Terry quarreled.

"I'll bring you dinner. Mrs. White's fried chicken. Come

on, Echo. I'll take you upstairs. Get you settled in." He gave her his smile.

It was his ace in the hole. When they went upstairs, he talked to her about her own hopes, hugged her with his heart and his hands and his eyes, and let her drift off with her head on his arm.

The sun was setting when she awoke and found her hand, which she thought held Max, embracing the ghost hand of the black scar on the floor. She shrank away, shut her eyes. And when she heard a familiar rasping sound and Max's low voice, she sat up.

He was sitting under the window at the far end of the room practicing his fingering on an electric guitar. He had no amp, of course, and the guitar looked pretty beat up, but he was bent over it, whispering his accompaniment. He was wearing a walkman she'd never seen before, and she realized he was listening to the tape Daniel/Perry had given her. It was the first time she'd seen Max intent on anything besides drugs since they'd moved to LA. She listened carefully, made out "Stairway to Heaven," of all things, and joined him on the lyrics.

He looked up and smiled, and she felt better than she had in weeks. She noticed he had changed into a sleeveless shirt.

They messed around with the play list, Max making just enough noise on the metal strings for Echo to get a sense of the rhythm. Soon it was dark, the moon rising behind Max, and then they heard Terry shouting from out front that a cab somebody had ordered was here and didn't plan on waiting for more than thirty seconds, on account of the *Bakana* starting up across the street. Max threw on a jean jacket and Echo wiggled into a long black t-shirt that would serve as a mini-dress, and they were out the door.

The parking lot of Chez Blues was packed when the cab pulled up on Sunset. Echo suspected that the staff filled the lot with their own cars, so everyone else would have to pay for valet parking. As she paid the cab driver, she wondered briefly where Max had gotten the money for the guitar. Her real distress, though, was that she heard a crowd inside, but no sound of musicians warming up.

The bouncer at the door eyed Max, who was pretty clearly underage, but when he pulled the guitar from the cab and slouched toward the entrance, the bouncer looked the other way.

Daniel was up on stage, talking urgently to a bass player and a keyboard man. When he saw the two newcomers, a wave of emotion broke across his face. Echo studied him carefully, to see how he'd react to Max with his guitar. He'd never really said Max was going to play tonight, and she was certain Daniel wouldn't have mentioned him to the rest of the band.

After a second, Daniel smiled and gestured them up on stage. "Echo this is Bad Billy Bass and Eighty-Eight Fingers. Max, man, good to see you."

"Daniel—"

"Perry. I'm Perry, okay?"

Max gave him a wry smile, clapped him on the shoulder, and said, "Good to see you, Perr."

"This *kid* is supposed to fill in for Jet?" Bad Billy interrupted. His arms were so cramped with tattoos they were nearly the same color as his sleeveless black leather vest. His face was creased and unfriendly, and a flat black Gaucho hat hid his eyes.

"He's good," Daniel protested. "One of the best I've ever heard."

"Nice pen and pin work, man," Max said, nodding toward

Bad Billy's prison artwork.

"We'll see," Billy said, turning away.

Echo smiled at the keyboard player, until he leered back at her. She turned toward Max and rolled her eyes.

Taking the two of them aside, Daniel said, "Glad you brought the ax, man. Our lead is MIA, but his amps are here." He talked about the rest of the play list. "If you guys can't do it, just fake. Don't know if the A&R people are gonna be here tonight, but if anybody asks, you guys were scheduled to try out and Jet just took the night off. That motherfucker."

Max plugged in and tuned up, Bad Billy silently watching him test the amp. When Max pulled off his jacket and was strapping on the guitar, Billy marched straight over to Daniel's drum kit and said loudly enough for half the bar to hear, "We've got a junkie sitting in for a junkie? Fucking great."

Daniel looked startled. Max shrugged and smiled, and suddenly let his fingers loose over the strings, ripping the air with a Stevie Ray Vaughan riff. Echo was the only one prepared for it, though Daniel should have been and recovered quickly.

You were supposed to wait for everybody to fiddle around with their instruments, to cross and curse themselves, to bitch about the sound system and grumble Who The Fuck Stole All My Picks? And you were supposed to wait for the recorded music to fade out and for an announcer to clue the crowd that a band, a bunch of *artistes* deserving their attention, was preparing for the difficult task of entertaining them for a few hours.

Fuck that. Max's guitar screamed "Scuttle Buttin'." He moved up to the front of the stage, where he stood, legs apart, young muscles rippling in the sleeveless red shirt, a small smile of shared pleasure shining out from his blond pretty-boy face. Daniel picked up the heavy back-beat, while

Bad Billy and Fingers simply gaped, astonished, slower to react even than the audience. Echo started hopping around on the stage, and as the crowd started dancing, Max pulled up short and (fuck the play list too) swung into the slightly slower "Cold Shot." Echo was at the mike on the other side of the stage, and when she opened up with a throaty, rasping, "Once was a sweet thing, baby," heads swivelled like they were trying to follow a car wreck. Bad Billy and Fingers got on-board, and the audience went wild.

"You know anything besides Stevie Ray?" Bad Billy sneered as they wound down under the audience applause six minutes later.

"I'm tryin' to make you feel at home," Max smiled.

"They'll love you in prison."

"On or off your play list?" Max asked.

"Let's do something I've practiced for a change." And he cranked into the bass lead on a Robert Cray song that Echo was all over in about two seconds, picking up on how Bad Billy was finding the ragged edges of the smooth song, clipping and shredding the lyrics until they fell on the room like burning confetti. They did some post-punk from the play list. Echo ripped on a Jack-Off-Jill song. Then Max took over, ending the set with another Stevie Ray Vaughan tune, "The Things That I Used to Do."

They were off the stage before anyone thought to introduce each other to the audience. Apparently that was a Jet thing, like cutting the stash or dividing the cash. The manager of the little club quickly rushed up on stage to assure everyone that NREmission would be right back after a *short* break.

"Where'd you get that Texas blues shit from, man," Daniel asked, clapping Max on the shoulder when they got over to their big corner table to towel off.

"Well, it's a jeans and t-shirt crowd," Max shrugged.

Daniel laughed and Fingers pursed his lips over teeth that reminded Echo of the giant sand-mouth sucking down Jabba's ship in one of the *Star Wars* movies. "This is LA, man," Daniel said. "T-shirts and jeans are what the *yuppies* wear. But you rocked 'em. You fuckin' rocked 'em anyway."

The five of them sat around the big table as the place closed. "I missed you, man," Max told Daniel over his beer.

"I don't know what's happening tomorrow morning," Bad Billy said. "Jet'll probably be pissed. But this was a fucking great night."

"Wasn't sure if you were comin' on board with "Scuttle Buttin'," Max grinned as they packed their cigarettes into their jacket pockets. "I guess it's true what they say about your reflexes going to hell when you hit twenty-one."

"Horseshit. That song was playing on the intercom when I knocked over my first convenience store, is all. I got sentimental for a minute."

They moved out into the night. When Daniel heard the unthinkable, that they were living in LA without a car, he offered to drive Max and Echo home, and Max was about to accept, when a voice behind them, a voice of someone who must have been leaning against the side of the door for a while, smoking a cigarette, waiting patiently for a sure thing, said, "It's okay. I know where they live."

Echo thought she'd seen the guy before, but couldn't remember where, which made no sense, 'cause he was sweet. Mid-twenties, tall, dark curls, Elvis eyes.

"Michael," Max said.

"Wanted to see how you did with that guitar," he smiled. "It never sounded like that before."

"It's a good, solid ax."

The man named Michael shook his head. "Keep it. I just

quit playing. But I'll still give you guys a ride back to the Park."

Max agreed, and Daniel waved off with the rest of the band. Echo heard Bad Billy mumble, way too loud, "Fuckin' cop." She was thinking, So that's where he got the guitar. And wondering, did that make her feel good or not?

11

Here in postmodernism's backseat boudoir
everyone loves the sinner
who lets him.

—Max

Max introduced Echo to Michael, told her he was someone trying to stop the murders in Echo Park. They exchanged looks, and Michael explained to Max, "I came by once, told Echo I was looking for my ex-girlfriend. That, uh, wasn't really true." He raised his left hand to display his wedding ring so she could see it from the back seat of the Taurus.

Echo nodded, apparently buying the straight-cop-inno-cently-befriending-the-kid-who-can-be-saved routine.

Max said, "Terry didn't tell me anything. But he's sup-posed to get me a sample of this E^2. I'll bring it by Bennies tomorrow, around one. It's been weird. People talk about E^2 in religious terms, even though they know it sometimes kills. Kind of like Russian Roulette. If Bakas decrees, you die. If not, you get the rush of your life. In the park, I can get any-thing except that shit. Like everyone's been warned not to sell it to me."

Michael looked alarmed, glanced toward Echo in the rear-view mirror.

"She won't say anything," Max told him. "Literally. Be-sides, I trust her more than I trust myself."

"Is it possible people in the 'hood know you're checking around for me? Maybe your friend Jumpin' Jack told them."

"Nah, how would Jack know? Terry's the only one I talked to. Besides, who'd believe anything coming from a junkie?"

The *Bakana* had broken up, but there were handfuls of

people still in the streets. Michael was looking for a bare stretch where they could slip out of the car discreetly, when they heard a scream. He jammed into the curb. "Wait till everyone's looking at me, and then get out," he told them. He exited the car and opened the back door a crack for them. A second later he had his gun out and was gone.

Echo got out first, Max right behind her. Max walked directly toward the crowd gathering twenty yards ahead, calling Echo to follow, caught up in a current rushing him away from her. She chased him, caught his arm. "It'll be okay," he whispered. "Just act like you don't know Michael."

The people who had gathered to witness the spectacle formed a semicircle around a graffitied wall. A young black man dressed in the usual gangster attire was on the ground, twitching horribly. Michael stood over him, gun still drawn, looking as horrified and awestruck as everyone else in the little crowd. The twitching man was glowing, as if his blood were red hot, glowing so bright Max could see it through the guy's clothes.

Michael pulled a cell phone from his back pocket and called for an ambulance. Max thought he should have called for back-up too. He was on the street in hostile territory, alone and deep into the night. But the crowd showed no sign of aggression; in fact, they reminded Max of a congregation gathered at a New Orleans funeral, an impression enhanced by a young woman standing next to him mumbling "Sweet Jesus."

But the man beside her said, "Praise Bakas," and a moment later, others in the crowd took up that chant as they watched the twitching man, his skin now moving strangely, coming and going in places, so that one minute Max was sure he was staring at a glowing, contorted arm, and the next at nothing. The smell started to get to him, and he pulled Echo away from the scene and back down the street toward their apartment. She was shaking violently the whole way, and it didn't stop when they got inside. Max laid her down on the air mattress that was their newest possession, and lay between her and the black stain-man on the floor, whom they'd taken to calling Casper. He held her until they both drifted off to the sounds of sirens.

Michael was sipping coffee in a booth when Max arrived at Bennies. Michael ordered him a cup. "Well?"

"You mean we don't go into the bathroom to make the exchange?"

Michael grinned and held out his hand and Max handed over a single black tablet with a hole in the middle. "Jesus, a little black donut?"

"The Cheerio of death," Max said. "One pill makes you larger, and one pill makes you small. Don't know which one that is."

"'White Rabbit?' That song came out probably twenty years before you were born."

"I know all the songs about drugs."

A waitress brought Max a cup and filled it.

"Your prints came back negative," Michael said.

"I'm so proud. Now if I could say as much for my AIDS test."

"You're positive for AIDS?"

"That's on a need to know basis. Tell me about your family. You're not wearing the ring today. Does that mean you fool around?"

As a cop, Michael was used to asking the questions, but Max watched him decide to talk. "Married to my high school sweetheart. Two kids, boy three and girl five."

"House in the suburbs? Two cars, if you count a Taurus as

a car?"

Michael shook his head. "LA cops have to live in the city. We're municipal employees. Where'd you learn to play guitar?"

Show me yours, I'll show you mine, Max thought, and told him a little about New Orleans.

"Echo from there too?"

"Only for the past year or so."

"You two . . . married?"

Max shook his head, but there was a tension in his denial that he himself couldn't ignore. "I don't want a . . . relationship. She does. I won't be her lover, because I care about her. Does that make sense?"

Michael nodded slightly. "Most cops are excitement junkies. You have . . . encounters, but when someone cares about you, shit will happen. So you try to stay away from those people."

"Even though that's the only real thing . . . "

"Even though."

They drank their coffee.

"You like your life?" Max asked.

"Yeah, I think so. What about you?"

"I don't know, don't know that I *could* know. It's like being color-blind. Maybe I'm just pretending to have a good time. Maybe everybody's pretending. A conspiracy of non-happy fools."

Michael looked at him, looked into his coffee, looked out the window . . . realized he was looking everywhere but into himself. "So how do you live? I mean, what are your rules?"

"I grew up selling myself," Max replied. "I know I can be bought." He smiled. "So I pride myself on my price. And on not charging it sometimes." He tapped his empty coffee cup on the table and picked up the black pill, fingered it wistfully.

"Thing is, if I don't take it, how can I tell Terry what it was like?"

"What do other people say? The ones who lived, I mean."

"That it's like E, only way better. Smoother, deeper."

"So tell him that."

"I hate saying what everybody else says."

Michael took the black pill from Max's hand, held it up briefly, then pocketed it. "Don't over-conceptualize it, Max. This shit is a bad thing."

"But it might be . . . an important bad thing. Like an affair, for instance."

Michael looked at him skeptically.

"Let's say you love your wife, but you cheat on her. If it's a meaningless affair and she finds out, you've screwed up. But what if it's not meaningless? What if it changes the way you are, the way you look at your life?"

"It's still bad; it's dishonest. You risk hurting people you care about, innocent people."

"But . . . this is your life. It's your only chance to feel, to see everything there is to see."

"To fuck everything there is to fuck?" Michael sneered.

"To fuck everything there is to fuck. At least one of every-thing, so you know. To know not so much about everything, but about yourself, about what things mean to you. About your ability to respond."

"No offense, but you sound like a seventeen-year-old Rim-baud on acid."

"Then why are you so afraid of your own bisexuality?"

Michael spewed coffee across the table.

Max went with Echo to the studio that afternoon and found Daniel waiting for them, apparently relieved to see them. "You forgot to give me a phone number," he said.

"Don't have one."

"Ah. Well, we found Jet. He's in detox. Can you play again tonight? Emergency gig. Can you believe it? A second record company wants to hear us before we sign!"

Max smiled and shrugged. "Is Bad Billy down with that?"

"Bad Billy is afraid of Jet, but he's greedy, just like I am. Suddenly we're looking at a potential bidding war instead of the usual one-disc contract. These A&R people don't know shit about what's good, but they know what's hot."

They rehearsed through the afternoon, and Billy, when he finally braced Max about Michael, was less hostile than he might have been.

"Your probation officer make you go down on him?"

"Nope. He's just making sure no bad-ass con is taking advantage of me."

In the end, Bad Billy was mollified by the news that Michael probably wouldn't be around that evening.

Chez Blues had been crowded the night before, but this evening it was packed. Which made it all the easier to identify the record company people, who had their own little table up front.

They started out with a Susan Tedeschi number and slid right into an alternative tune from Esthero, both featuring Echo. Max could feel the heat from a tall blond woman in a red dress at the A&R table and laid into her with a hard-edged version of a Dave Matthews song, "I Did It," that blew the doors down. When Daniel announced a couple of originals, the crowd was appreciative, and the A&R people approving (although until the Matthews song they'd never even moved in their chairs). Max tried not to look directly at the blond woman, which wasn't easy. Bad Billy backed up to him and grunted, "A&R people don't dance. Least I never saw it before."

During the break, the A&R people came over, dabbing at their unsightly sweat stains, and Daniel tried to explain Jet's absence and Max's ambiguous status with the band. The blond woman brought over a photographer and asked if she could take photos of Echo and Max, some together, some separate. She introduced herself as Lucy Something-that-sounded-like-Ricardo-but-couldn't-have-been. "Have you done any modeling?"

"Modeling?" Echo repeated, thinking of what the euphemism had meant in New Orleans.

"With the Powers Agency, maybe? You two look very GQ."

"We're just born posers," Max laughed.

"You have that Halle Berry thing going, and you . . . " She slid her hand along Max's shoulder, lingering along the back of his neck, pretending it was just for confidentiality's sake. "If we do this," she whispered, "I can see some big-time advertising work. A multimedia blitz. The two of you are going to be everywhere."

"If we do this?" Echo echoed.

The woman smiled and went to talk to Daniel. Max laughed at Echo's expression. "I know you'd hate moving out of Echo Park, but it might not be all bad."

Echo hugged him, started to climb all over him right there, until the appreciative crowd got them to take the heat back on stage.

The next day was Monday, and NRMission had the day off. Tuesday morning, Echo was back at the studio for back-up vocal work she'd scheduled the previous week. Max was sitting on the stoop talking to Terry, when Bad Billy pulled up in a classic Thunderbird. The man in the passenger seat had straight blond hair that went halfway down his back, a short blond goatee, the wired, fleshless arms of a serious junkie hanging from his white tank top. His dragon tattoos had some color in them, were less jailhouse than Bad Billy's. Bad Billy had to hurry to interpose himself between Max and the new man.

"You must be Jet," Max said before anyone else spoke. "I was hoping you'd get back soon."

"I'll bet," Jet snarled.

"When I'm strung out, I usually like a Percocet. You want one? Terry, you got any Percocet? Jet here is trying to get his shit together."

Bad Billy was pretending to look across the street at the park, at the graffiti on the buildings, at the street kids who were looking at his car in a way he didn't like, which was any way at all. Terry thought about the Percocet, then produced one, as he seemed able to produce just about anything from the dozen little pockets inside his shabby brown overcoat. He held it out to Jet, who took a close look at him for the first time.

"Shit. What happened to your eyes, man?"

"They saw what they weren't supposed to see," the Snake replied. "They still do."

Jet took the pill and swallowed it dry. "Yeah, whatever." He turned his attention back to Max. "I hear you did a hell of a job filling in for me while I was, uh, sick. I appreciate that. But the gig's over. You got that?"

"Sure," Max shrugged. He looked over at Bad Billy and caught him staring. "Nice wheels, man."

Bad Billy grimaced, but finally spoke. "Thanks for helping out, man, you were great. I mean, you were good."

"Now the girl," Jet said, wetting his lips, "we might be able to use her."

"I'll let her know," Max nodded. "She's got, uh, Perry's number."

"I wanna see her."

"She's not here."

Finally meeting resistance, if only imagined resistance, Jet seemed more in his element, and stepped closer, too close. Max had to look up at him from crotch level. "Well, where is she?"

"She's working," Max said. Then: "You sure that was a Percocet you gave him, Terry?" Suddenly Max was lighting a clove, his Bic flame two inches high and about an inch from Jet's pants. Jet jumped back but balled his fists up.

The blind man thought it over. "He *is* kind of jumpy. It wasn't a black pill, was it, with a hole in the middle?"

Jet slapped the clove from Max's mouth and hauled him to his feet with a handful of t-shirt. Cursing, Bad Billy stepped into it. "Let him go, Jet. The kid's solid. If he says he'll tell her, he'll tell her."

With a hard stare, Jet let go, stalked back to the car. A minute later they were gone.

"So much for fame and fortune," Max frowned, having retrieved the clove and found it broken.

Terry said, "I don't think it's gonna be *that* easy for you to amount to nothin'."

"Maybe it's for the best. I was struggling with divided loyalties. What else do you have besides Percocets?"

Terry turned his head toward the empty street. "Michael's coming. Alone, this time."

12

The dead give bad head.
—Max

Echo returned that evening, not in a cab, but in a black limousine. The driver waited while she ran upstairs with a package. Reaching the landing just below her apartment, she caught her breath and stopped. There were two blackened souls on the floor, new ones, seemingly struggling with each other; and one more on the wall. She remembered the scene on the street the other night, remembered too what Juno had told her about magic being a force like gravity, and knew these thoughts were somehow connected, as if someone could get sucked into a black hole in reality.

She staggered up the last flight of stairs to the apartment, the package still under her arm. Max was just coming out of the shower, groggy but basically sober. She gestured toward the little window at the end of the narrow apartment, got Max to look out at the limousine.

"I don't steal cars." he said. "Neither of us can drive."

Echo pulled a new dress from her package and tossed the rest to Max.

"If you want these thrown out the window, you'll have to do it yourself; I kind of like them," he grinned, pulling a shiny gray tank top and matching parachute pants from the bag. Then he looked out at the limo again. "Those the A&R people from the other night?" Echo already had stripped off her jeans and t-shirt and was shimmying into the gray dress, made from the same material as Max's clothing. He followed suit and they were headed back downstairs a minute later, Echo trying to fuss with Max's hair while he dodged her on the staircase.

The driver, a tall black man in livery, was waiting by the door of the limo, his hands crossed in front of him, pretending not to stare at Terry, who was smiling at him with his broken teeth. Lucy, the tall blond woman from Chez Blues, wearing a similar but different red dress, was alone in the back seat. She extended her hand to Max and pulled him forward for a peck on the cheek. Then, as the limo started up, she inspected both of them. "That is perfect!" she crowed. "Jean-Carlo is going to love you. How long did it take you to get your hair like that, Max?"

"All afternoon."

"Well, don't lose that look!"

Echo rolled her eyes.

"Where are we going?" Max laughed.

"Dinner. What's your favorite restaurant?"

"Bennies. I mean, that Denny's on the other side of the park." Echo elbowed him, and he added, "We like Cajun food. We spent a lot of time in New Orleans."

Lucy frowned. "Perry said you knew each other from New York."

"After that," Max nodded.

"But you look so young. You *are* eighteen, aren't you? You have to be that old to sign a legal contract in California."

Echo and Max exchanged looks. "Sure," Max said. "We just don't have ID. Our apartment was burglarized."

Lucy nodded sympathetically. "I shouldn't wonder. I'll see about getting that replaced for you. Oh, and Echo tells me you're not represented?"

"No. I mean, yes, we're not represented. But we're way older than eighteen."

Lucy briefed them about dinner. She was not in A&R, she explained, but was with a major agency. She said that this was better for them, because, if they had signed with a label un-represented, they would have been totally ripped off. Plus, she had contacts throughout "The Industry," which wasn't just the music industry, but the entertainment industry. They were meeting with both a record producer and a client of hers from a modeling agency at dinner. "Sorry about forcing these clothes on you." She wrinkled up her nose. "But the client will want to convince himself you're really into his line. It's called GrungeWear, by the way." Her expression suggested it was no worse than a lot of other hip Gap imitators.

Echo prayed Max wouldn't mention that they didn't have anything else to wear anyway. He didn't. He asked Lucy about their friend Perry. "He's an old friend, the one who brought us in for that gig. We'd like to give him a try as drummer."

Lucy looked briefly tired, but masked it with a shrug and a smile. "Does he have an agent?"

"I don't think so."

"If you want him, I'll be glad to talk to him."

Echo nudged Max, so he persisted. "He's a good drum-mer."

"So are a lot of better looking, more dynamic kids. But maybe that's okay. I see the two of you fronting for a bunch of highly skilled but essentially invisible pros. Like, uh, the Eurythmics. If you want him, have him call me."

Echo thought about that a moment, realized Lucy wasn't interested in signing up a whole band with an original artistic vision, but in packaging and promoting a product. Well, what was the problem? Wasn't her greatest talent to be whomever somebody else wanted her to be?

Lucy opened a cabinet set into the back of the driver's seat, revealing a small refrigerator. "A drink to relax before we make our big entrance?" she suggested. "And, oh," she added, as if noticing the folder on top on the unit for the first time, "of course, the contracts. You'll have to sign them if I'm going to negotiate anything tonight."

Echo looked at Max, who grinned back. They both signed. He took a Scotch and Echo indicated a beer but took a white wine when Lucy explained that's what people would expect of her from now on.

From Now On. After dinner, when the clothing manufacturer and the record company had both signed them up for more money than she could imagine (even with Max assuring her that Lucy would probably make sure they never saw most of it), Echo started counting time from this new ground zero. She wondered where they'd all be in, say, the year 5, *FNO*.

She could not have guessed, of course, although, while at the busy restaurant with its outrageous *chichi* social rituals, she had only to close her eyes to see, on the inside of her lids, a weird *chiaroscuro* of the same scene, in which she had become an enormous, bloated Hive Queen attended, cleaned, milked, impregnated, and fed by a cadre of buzzing, faceless drones. Frighteningly, in her vision, Max was nowhere to be seen.

You close your eyes and you wake up in a whole new world. They did a photo shoot the next day, Lucy paying a fortune for each of them to sit in front of blazing lights with a cloth backdrop for head shots and then, in a somewhat larger room and wearing a variety of clothing, for the rest of what Lucy called their "portfolio." Echo brought an apprehensive, girl/woman sexual vulnerability to the photo shoot, apologizing in anticipation of disaster, as might a deer caught in the headlights of a Mack truck for scraping chrome off the grill. Then she realized the photographer was smiling so hard the skin on his frequently lifted face was nearly cracking. It was "mahvelous," he said. He hadn't seen anything like it in years. These days, even child models affected such blasé world-weariness that he was "absolutely *positivo*" this new look, *The Echo Look*, would "just slay."

Because he also was shooting Max, who was able to display such a variety of seductive, questioning, bad boy, or gutter angel poses at the drop of a suggestion, the photographer was *positivo* Echo had spent years perfecting her look and was simply stringing him along.

Later that evening, choosing the shots to use in their portfolios was far more fun. Lucy actually did most of the choosing, allowing Max and Echo their "input" as one might one's children in a restaurant before ignoring their "french fries and banana split" orders.

Echo's favorite photo was one that showed Max in his bad boy pose, eyes wide, a dark brown clove in his slightly extended hand, smoke curling to one side of his face, the side unable to contain a smile at Echo, who was seated at his feet and hugging one of his knees, one thin arm mysteriously invisible because she had snaked it up the inside leg of his pants. Lucy nixed it, because it didn't fit with The Look she wanted, but Echo kept the proofs.

Ironically, the photo Lucy liked best was the straight version of the same pose, Max brooding through smoke-pursed lips with Echo clinging protectively to his legs. When Echo saw the photo months later, on a Sunset Strip billboard advertising a promotional gig at the Whisky for the CD *Echo and Narcissus*, she shook Max awake, Max who had been nodding off on her shoulder.

"We have a CD?" he asked dreamily. "Is it any good?"

Technically, they moved to a Beverly Hills bungalow the following week. It was cozy and unprepossessing, and cost as much to rent for a month as it would have to buy the same house back in Athens. But Max seemed to forget where he lived, and more than once when he didn't show up for a rehearsal or a photo shoot, Echo found him back in Echo Park, on the stoop, talking to Terry. He'd look at his wrist— although he never wore a watch—and climb into the back of the limo or cab with her. Sometimes she could tell he had been shooting horse. But on Max, dissolution looked so hip that eventually it became a national advertising craze.

Echo didn't know why Echo Park held such gravitational power over them. Sometimes it reminded her of a cartoon she'd seen in which all the people of the world were being sucked down a giant drain at the bottom of the ocean. The ghosts of long-drowned sailors, unaffected by the irresistible swirl in the living dimension, simply went about their business, unaware that the world was ending.

13

*I'm not interested in a future with you
or with me.*

—Max

Max watched Michael try to light a cigarette. The first match didn't catch, nor the second. Max lit his clove in one smooth motion, took the cigarette from Michael's lips, and used the clove as a coal for it. "What?"

"I never did anything like that before."

"Never had a blow job?"

"I never did anything like *that* before."

Max blew the smoke away from in front of his face. "With a guy, you mean?"

"Yeah."

Max studied him for a minute. "You don't even want to look at me right now, you're so pissed off at yourself. Look at me."

Michael exhaled, then finally swung his gaze to Max.

Max smiled at him with affection and watched the muscles in Michael's face relax. "Remember now why it's okay?"

"It's *not* okay."

"You did it because you felt something for me and maybe I felt something for you. You didn't hurt anybody."

"But I'm not . . . that's not who I am." But he kept staring at Max. "That's not who I *was*."

"If it bothers you, go back and *be* who you were. You can. No one will ever know."

Michael looked at him, looked at him, stubbed out his cigarette without looking down at it. "Does it hurt?"

"A little. Especially if you wear a rubber."

"What if I don't?"

"I'm HIV positive, Michael. No, I don't have AIDS. Hell, I never even get a cold; Terry says it's part of my magic. But I could be contagious."

Michael nodded thoughtfully. He took the clove from Max's lips, pulled another cigarette from his shirt pocket, and lit it off the clove. "I appreciate that that's on a need-to-know basis."

Michael was tucking his shirt into his pants as they came out of the old apartment building; it wasn't until he had gotten into his copmobile that Max turned back and saw Echo. Flushed and perspiring, he walked up to the cab and flopped into the back seat next to her, leaning his head back on the seat where it abutted the door frame. When Echo did not come to him and put her head on his shoulder, he looked at her.

"You can't talk and I can't feel," he laughed drunkenly. "We're the perfect uncouple." He closed his eyes before adding, "I wasn't betraying you, Echo. I can't. I was betraying Terry."

"So why are you still living in this shithole?" Terry asked, the day after that first photo shoot.

Max shrugged. "We're kids, legally. We have to live somewhere people don't ask a lot of questions."

"You're taking it up the ass from that cop, Michael, is why you're still hanging around down here."

"Don't be such a romantic."

Terry actually smiled at that. "You're right. You're not that interested in anybody. You're fucking with him for a reason. Now why can't I see it?"

Max tried to control his expression. Maybe Terry couldn't

see his expressions, but he always seemed to feel them. "I like him. It's interesting. Unusual. He's so damn straight."

"He's dangerous. And so are you."

What the hell, Max thought. "He wants to find out who's behind this Bakas thing. To stop the murders. I'm trying to help him."

"Shit," Terry exhaled. "So that's why I can't see it."

"Huh? I don't follow you."

Terry was silent a moment, then said, "Those people who've died, who were they?"

"Well, there was Rufus, that bad motherfucker who needed braces. Maybe that's why he liked to bite his whores when they pissed him off. He was only like sixteen, maybe braces would have changed his disposition. Then there was—"

"Junkies, pimps, and dealers, that's who they were."

"Well, it's Needle Park. That's like generalizing about Republicans in the Midwest."

"Get serious!" Terry snapped.

"Okay. They were Crips, Bloods, and a lot of other low-lifes who wished they . . . " Max stared at Terry as he got it. "Good God."

"No, just the agent of one."

"You? But . . . how . . . ?"

"I once knew a generous man who refused to help anyone because he thought he might be giving a dollar to Satan, or at least to a killer who might use it to buy bullets. That's not my way."

"The pill you gave me, the cops analyzed it. It was nothing but high-grade Ecstacy."

"I know."

"We saw a guy who took the other kind. We didn't stay until the end. Michael says he just seemed to melt right into the ground."

"You ask Echo about what that is? No? Well, she can communicate with me, without words, and she knows more than them others. The burned people you can't figure out, they're like black holes. She tried singing to one, and her voice *goes in*, goes somewhere, but never comes out. No echo. You know what she asked me? 'Is this what a door to hell looks like, Mr. Terry?'"

"What do you want me to do, Terry?"

"If I tell you the Apocalypse is coming, you'll just think I'm crazy, right?"

"No. I just won't understand you."

Terry nodded. "Right. You deal in personal shit. So let me put it this way. Get yourself out of here. Go with Echo and live your new life."

"Beverly Hills just doesn't feel like my home town."

"There is someone coming for you here. Go now."

Max was sitting in the Taurus, listening. Michael was steering and talking. "The Mara Humara, I think they're called, a tribe of Indians from a place in Mexico called Copper Canyon. Mayans, who live in little villages in the Sierra Nevadas. All the villages are isolated, and the only way between one and the next is by foot, so running is a big part of the culture, maybe even of the religion. Everybody talks about the runners, aspires to be one, tells stories about great runs. The big sport is this three hundred mile relay where each team member runs a fourteen mile leg, several days in a row, kicking what looked to me like a croquet ball. Barefooted."

"You saw this on the S&M channel?"

"Discovery. It just seemed like it would be cool to live someplace where goals were a little tough, but were so clear-cut. If you can walk or run from one village to the next with your mailbag or whatever, you've had a good day. A satisfying day. Period. Of course, maybe on a bad day, you break your leg and starve, but you know when you get up in the morning that you only have to accomplish this one thing. No ambiguity, you know what I mean?"

"Hypothetically," Max said. "But we're not them. We've learned to be complicated and unhappy, and that's your nature now, and mine."

Michael nodded and pulled into the driveway of a fast food joint Max had never seen before.

"Buddha's Burgers? I thought Buddhists were vegetarians."

"Maybe that's why this is the only one."

"Must be good. Five bucks for a burger?"

"The burgers suck. That's not why we're here." Michael pulled up to an enormous papier mâché Buddha and spoke into the grid in its belly. "Hold the burger. I'm thinking of making a major change in my life."

"Five dollar. Pull up to the second window."

A middle-aged Thai woman was seated on a stool next to the register at the window. A plastic head-covering, designed to make her look bald, was pulled halfway back on her head. "Ah, Detective Mike. Five dollar." Michael handed her the Lincoln and she looked reflexively at both sides of it. She said, "Change is death." Then she began to shut the window.

"Ah," Michael interrupted quickly, "could you Supersize that answer?"

"You seek change as a solution to confusion. Might as well kill yourself now. That solve all your problems."

"How are the fries?" Max asked.

He figured Michael really wanted him to ask about the Big Change he, Michael, was contemplating, but Max had no intention of contributing to the delinquency of an adult. Instead, he reached into the back seat and pulled out an acoustic guitar, the one he still liked to compose on, and started plucking out notes in a twelve-bar blues pattern. He sang:

> *Pain is my home,*
> *and this needle is the key.*
> *Pain is my home,*
> *this guitar pick is the key.*
> *If you're coming home with me*
> *Don't think your dick's the key.*

Michael looked at him, his face a mask of shame and confusion.

The debut performance of Echo & Narcissus at the Whisky was a bit too much of a gala for Max, but then, in LA, you couldn't open a McDonald's without klieg lights and a parade. He wished Daniel were with them, because he would have appreciated this shit, but Daniel was trying to work things out with the original label he had contracted with, and also with Jet, who had threatened to kill him if he left the band.

"Jeez, did you dress in the dark?" Lucy snorted when she saw him.

"Could you be more specific?"

"Diagonal rows of pink and green monkeys on the tie don't go with the white and gray gondolas horizontal on the powder blue shirt."

"It's my spring line." Max pirouetted for her. "I call it Chaos. The Concept is riotous, fecund nature, coming alive after winter-long fashion dormancy when everyone was wearing the funereal Ralph Lauren, that George Plimpton wannabe. *Chaos: the Mother of All Patterns.* I'd explain further, but I have an appointment to get my blood changed."

"Lose the tie before you lose your sponsor. Kiss me for luck." She gave him a double LA air job. "You're on."

Echo opened with a Bjork number while Max played low-level havoc with the show-tune-styled music, turning his guitar into a one-man orchestra without distracting anyone from the vocals. They did a bunch of his original tunes, which were to be featured on the new CD, announced but not yet recorded. Lucy nodded approval over a glass of champagne—or was it a designer water with a twist?—from the end of the bar. The audience went wild no matter what they did, or how or when they did it. Max loved performing, but, to the extent he cared about audience response, this crowd pissed him off.

Echo must have sensed this, and pulled him aside after the first few numbers.

"The fucking record company must have paid a bunch of people to applaud," he explained. "This is no fucking fun."

"Fucking fun," Echo grinned at him.

Max got it, thought for a moment, and stepped back up to the microphone. "Okay, everybody who was paid by the record company, raise your hands." There was confusion and tittering from the crowd. "I mean it. We're not doing anything up here until we get this straightened out. Now, raise those hands."

Fully half the crowd eventually raised their hands.

Max sighed. "This is worse than I thought. Okay, all you paid people, take your disease over to that side of the room. What about the rest of you? Why are you here?"

"Free tickets!" someone shouted from the back.

"Shit. Well, at least you're free to leave whenever you want. How about the bartenders? The waitresses? What do you guys want to hear?" When no one answered, he tortured a few chords of "Stairway to Heaven." One woman on the Free Ticket side—Max thought he recognized her from Chez

Blues—started to laugh, and Max jumped off the low stage and strutted up to her with his guitar. Echo grabbed the mike. "Think I'm bluffing, huh?" He ripped off a huge chord and Echo sang, in a brief Robert Plant falsetto, as she walked down the steps to join him, "She's descend—ing a stairway to hell—ll," growling out of the falsetto on the last, extra syllable, and ripping into the old standard. They danced around the floor between the two groups, screaming, blaring, entwining in grotesque postures of tormented sexuality. By the time they finished, the entire club was roaring with approval.

When the first set ended, they went backstage to their first ever actual dressing room to towel off. Max had drunk three or four bottles of water during the set, and had sweated most of it out. He was in the bathroom pissing away the rest, when there was a commotion and Echo screeched. He shoved open the door and lunged through—only to be leveled by a blow to the forehead.

A moment later, when he opened his eyes, he found himself staring up at a big black man, who was holding Echo like an elongated football under one arm. Max remembered Terry's warning about someone coming to look for him.

"Officer Nemo," Max said, though without his usual smile, "I bet you have a request."

"Yeah, I do, smart boy." He looked down at Echo. "Did you know your boyfriend here was a fag? Do you know he seduces people just to fuck them up?"

Echo looked up at him, then down at Max in panic.

"It's the fag part you can't stomach, right?" Max said. "If he was having an affair with a lawyer's wife or getting it free from some hooker, like a normal cop, that'd be okay, right?"

"You fucked up my partner real good, and I'm thinking about doing the same to you." Nemo put one huge foot on Max's open fly and pressed down.

Groaning, Max grabbed the foot with both hands, but couldn't budge it.

"He was a nice family man, before you got your hooks into him. I liked that about him. I want him back that way. You got me?" He exerted a more noticeable pressure.

Someone was pounding on the door outside. "You're jealous?" Max groaned.

Nemo brought his foot back to kick, but in the split second Max could move again, he rolled to the side. Before the big cop could react, two security guards burst into the room and made straight for him. A brief melee ensued, in which Nemo released Echo so he could use both arms. She and Max scrambled behind a couch, where they stayed until the pandemonium receded down the hallway.

His eyes closed, Max leaned back against the couch, gasping. He could hear Echo doing the same. And he could also hear the audience calling for them. He looked at Echo; there were tears in her eyes. She reached up one slender arm and pulled him into an embrace. Then they rose together, and went back to the stage.

"This looks more like it," Max said as they emerged. He scanned the crowd, looking in vain for a particular face, thinking of Terry and of Michael, and of all the soul shadows that lay between them. "This is for someone I can't ever see again," he said into the microphone. He played the first chords of the old Queen Standard, "Bohemian Rhapsody," but sang instead, "All my tracks lead back to you/When at home/Do as the homos do."

Their debut CD, called simply *Echo and Narcissus*, was released while the ad campaign for GrungeWear was four-walling. It probably would have been a smash even if it hadn't been as good as it was, and it probably would have been less begrudgingly accepted in the music community if it hadn't been a smash.

It was an interesting time for Max, because he rather enjoyed people's ambivalence. It was a hopeful time for Echo, because she was spending more sober-time with Max. It was *not,* however, a good time for the people in Echo Park.

Max found this out one night when he was leaving a television studio after a live interview, and discovered his limo driver embroiled in a heated discussion with two uniformed policemen. Not sure what sort of drug paraphernalia might be stuck in the various rear compartments of the vehicle, he was watching from a safe distance when a Taurus pulled up beside him. Michael was alone. He gestured for Max to climb in the passenger side.

"Okay," Max said. "Just get your buddies to let my driver go."

"I can't really . . . get involved," Michael replied.

"You're drinking on duty now?" Max smelled the alcohol, and gave Michael a closer look.

"Too old fashioned for you?"

"I'd call it quaint. You've lost weight." Michael's eyes were hollow, and he was unkempt and unshaven. In fact, he had come to look like a darker version of Max himself.

Max got in. "You look like shit, dude."

"And you lack a certain moral authority, on this and other subjects." Michael sighed and looked out the side window as they pulled out of the lot.

"Hey, I meant that as a compliment."

Michael smiled faintly and looked over at him. "You look like shit yourself. The difference is, on you it looks good."

Max made a noncommittal gesture and glanced casually at his side-view mirror, wondering if Michael had made sure Nemo wasn't following him. Cops were supposed to be on top of that stuff, but Michael seemed distracted. "What's happening back at the Park?"

"Hmm? Well, more deaths, a lot more. So many that potential users are backing off. It's gotten too dangerous even for *those* macho bastards, like playing Russian Roulette with three bullets in the gun instead of one."

So he still doesn't know it's Terry, Max thought, doesn't understand this is the Snake's revenge against everyone who hurt him, including the cops, who'll never have any credibility in a 'hood where they can't solve a hundred related murders. "So you think I can do something about it? Make a public service announcement or something? The D.A.R.E. people were talking to me about that the other day. They said I had tremendous clout in the drug community. I said, yeah, I always pay up front, with cash."

"I want you back."

Max looked at him, then joined him in staring out the windshield. "Michael, your partner threatened to kill me, not to mention Echo, if I came near you again. This conversation probably counts as a capital offense in his book. He's not dead, is he?"

"Sorry, no."

"Not to mention your wife, the high school sweetheart, and your kids."

"I'll leave them. The cops and my family."

Max sucked in his breath and exhaled slowly. "Hey, take it easy."

"I could be your body guard. Head of security, whatever. You're going to be touring soon, right? We'd be out of LA. No one would bother us."

Max forced himself to look at his former lover. "You've got a lot of guts, Michael. I admire the hell out of you. I care about you. But didn't we decide before we started that that's exactly the kind of affair neither of us wanted to have?"

"You're afraid to get close to me because of the HIV thing, that's what I think. You're afraid to get close to anyone because of that."

"It's a reason."

"Not with me."

"Now don't give me that, Michael. I could kill you. I spread death. Get it?"

"I've got a bullet lodged in my spine. One bad step some day, and I could paralyze myself. It doesn't stop me from walking."

"Michael, you have a wife and kids. Go back to them."

"I don't even know where they are." He was wild-eyed, and Max couldn't figure out what he meant. "I mean, they're probably back at the house. But in my head, they're not there. You're the only one there."

Max put his hand on Michael's shoulder, felt a jolt of current. And he felt how emaciated Michael was becoming. "I'm sorry. It's not like that for me. I don't think I can feel that way."

"So it's not just Nemo?"

"Nemo was a catalyst, that's all. Hell, he was even right for a change. You were a great guy being who you were. You—"

"But that's *not* who I am. Knowing you has changed me."

Max put his head back on the seat. "So you're gonna chuck your shoes and run through the Sierra Nevadas? Go back. You don't have to be fucked up. You're basically a straight guy." Somehow he recognized the sound he heard in response: the gun sliding from Michael's shoulder holster. He turned his head and saw the cop with his pistol pressed to his own temple. "Hey, isn't there a law against doing that while you're driving?"

"'Boredom kills. Just ask God.' You still think that?" But

Micheal wasn't trading quips. In a fraction of a second, Max saw the look in his eye and the finger tightening on the trigger. He swung his left fist backhand at the gun, fast and hard, made contact just as the bullet exploded from the chamber.

The car swerved. Max felt the pain in his hand and heard Michael's scream as the front of the car smashed into something, throwing both men against the windshield, and kept moving, through three or four more jolts before it stalled out.

Pulling himself back into his seat, Max looked over at Michael. There was blood trickling down his scalp, but his eyes were open and he seemed more or less oriented.

"You'd better get out of here," Michael gasped. "I'll say I was questioning an unknown suspect."

Max looked for the gun, saw it in Michael's lap.

"It's okay. I promise. Get out of here."

Max pulled open the door, squeezed between the parked cars against which they had come to rest, and limped down the street. His head was bleeding and his hand was burning, but for once no one seemed to notice him.

14

The bruise learns the necessity of lies.
                                        —Max

Echo looked over the rusted railing down toward the basement apartment where Terry supposedly lived. She was looking for Max, who'd missed rehearsal again. No light seeped around the doorway, but what did that tell you about a blind man being home?

She was hesitant to go down to the creepy-looking place until a car she didn't like the looks of squealed around the corner and headed toward her. Scampering down the stairs and out of sight, she heard car doors slamming and voices above.

"That bitch is singing with us."

A voice she recognized as Bad Billy's answered. "She don't *belong* to us, Jet. We only asked her to try out because Perry was so hot on her—"

"Fuck Perry. She sings with us, or she don't sing at all."

Having heard enough, Echo pushed on Terry's door; it swung open, and she stepped in without waiting to be invited.

That step seemed to carry her into a different environment, like a steam room or a walk-in freezer, except that what she felt had nothing to do with hot or cold, was more like what she'd felt that evening on the bank of the Mississippi, when Juno had asked her to look for love.

"Miss Echo?" When he spoke, she saw him through darkness that only a moment before had seemed impenetrable. He was sitting in an enormous old torn and sprung armchair, an armchair big as a throne, a throne for the King of the Dump.

He'd either been asleep or deep in thought, and for the first time Echo could recall, seemed surprised. "Miss Echo," he said again, and she realized it wasn't surprise but recognition and resignation. "Welcome to the Apocalypse." Terry grunted at his own pretension. "Usually it's the young telling the old the world is gonna end. The old been through that already. Mostly we complain about entropy. Know what that is? Don't matter. But I got to tell you, child, something big is gonna happen here in Echo Park. You can feel that, can't you?"

Don't stop talking, she thought. You know why I'm here.

"I'd ask you why you're here," Terry said, "except I know better than you do. You're looking for someone. Someone's looking for you."

"You bet your ass, old fart," Jet said through the doorway. Echo hadn't closed the door all the way and the nasty-looking, long-haired blond man, all wires and edges, pushed it open.

Gasping, backing into the room, Echo saw Bad Billy behind Jet, but he looked away from her supplicating glance. Jet hesitated on the threshold.

"That's right, white boys. I didn't say for you to come in. And you can't, 'less I say," Terry cackled.

Jet tried to step forward; somehow his step took him off to the side, not through the door. He tried again, traveled every which way except into the room. "What the fuck?!"

Billy said, "Just ask her, then let's go."

"Ask her?" Jet seemed dumbfounded by the concept. "Okay, bitch, you wanna come sing for us, or you want I pop a cap up your fag friend's ass while I teach you how to fuck?"

Billy sighed.

"Is this the guy that writes the lyrics?" Terry said. "No wonder your band's no good."

"Shut the fuck up old man. You can't hide in there forever."

"My, my. I thought you wanted me to invite you in. That's how it works, you know. Like with vampires."

"Or cops without a warrant," Billy added. "Let's get out of here, Jet. Just tell her where we'll be, and she'll come if she wants to."

"Fuck that. You gonna invite me in, old man?"

Echo looked wildly about the dark recesses of the room for a weapon or a window or door to jump out of. Even if Terry's apartment was warded, like Juno's house had been, she'd seen what could happen once the door was breached.

Jet followed her glance suspiciously. "And put on a light while you're at it."

"Come on in," Terry said, sliding from his throne and advancing with his cane to the middle of the room. "Sure I can't offer you another pill, Mr. Jet?"

"I heard about your damn pills." He took a step forward and this time succeeded in crossing the threshold. "Get a light on in here," he commanded.

"The switch is next to the door." Terry pointed at a dark patch in a very dark wall.

Jet reached out a hand tentatively and then drew it back. "That looks like bare wires to me, old man."

"I don't have much cause to use it," Terry smiled. His eyes swirled madly, in a way Echo hadn't noticed before. When she realized what was going to happen, she bolted for the door.

Jet's slap caught her on the side of her head, sent her crashing into the doorjamb, and as she bounced off, he grabbed her by the hair and bent her over backwards until she was staring up at him. "You're gonna sing now, or you're gonna sing later. Or maybe both."

Echo heard the whistle of Terry's cane and its crack against Jet's flesh. "You old fuck," Jet cursed. He threw Echo out the door, into Bad Billy's arms. But even as Jet took another step forward into the darkened room, Terry stepped back, disappeared into the dark.

From outside the room, only a few feet away, Echo could barely make out Jet's white t-shirt and blond hair. Then, from nowhere, Terry appeared, his back to her, facing Jet, his free hand next to the bare wires.

"You want light, Mr. Jet? I'll show you the light." As Jet spun toward him, Terry pointed his cane at the man's chest and grabbed the wires.

The room was flooded with a blinding incandescence, flowing through Terry and out the tip of his cane, across to where Jet stood, now burning like a neon tube.

Echo screamed back the sound of that light. Billy managed only a choking sound. In a moment, the brilliance subsided, but an eerie glow remained.

"Jesus H. Christ," Billy said, and Echo thought he was praying to the wrong god. She went back inside before the light could fade completely. The room was empty, save for the big, ragged chair, and, lying on the floor, Terry's cane. Where Jet had stood, only black footprints remained.

They considered cancelling the gig scheduled for that night. Except for a slightly swollen face where she'd hit the doorjamb, Echo was surprisingly unscathed, and Max told her the swelling made her look artsy, kind of like a Picasso painting, lopsided woman, half-haunted sexuality, half-bruised maternity. "Modern Woman," he called her, and she couldn't help laughing. Max's hand, though, was swollen from powder burns, and his head was throbbing where he had cracked it against the windshield.

Problem was, this was the highly publicized sendoff show at the Whisky A Go-Go, starting the Echo and Narcissus Tour. They were going to be touring with highly competent, eclectic studio musicians, particularly the keyboard player, second guitar, and bass. Echo paged Lucy, who brought in a doctor to treat Max's injuries, and, almost absentmindedly, leave exactly the combination of pills he'd need to get through the evening's performance. Lucy asked if he'd be okay for their opening at the Hard Rock Hotel in Vegas in three days. The doctor shrugged, said that depended on what Max did to himself in the meantime.

Daniel—or rather Perry—finally had come back on board after Jet had failed to show for yet another gig. Echo thought the new LA look and manner Daniel affected were laughable, but that he was basically a damn nice guy who could have had any number of serious girlfriends, if he didn't waste his time lavishing his attentions on her. Whenever they were on stage together, Echo could feel him watching her, nearly hypnotized, until she might have screamed with frustration—if she weren't just as obsessed with Max. How ironic, she thought, that the only hope they had for a meaningful conversation would be to talk about their complete lack of hope for any meaningful relationship.

Max made it through the first set, swollen hand and all, though Echo could tell he was limping by the end and made up for it by taking over center stage and running a capella vocal riffs where Max ordinarily might offer a spontaneous guitar solo. He was playing every other note, and with none of his usual pyrotechnics, but he kept smiling and the crowd kept loving him. (Echo wondered if Lucy had salted the crowd, giving her people specific instructions, duh, not to raise their hands if Max asked.) Echo closed the set very down

and dirty with an old blues standard about a woman on the
way to the electric chair for killing her husband. Max pretended to fall mortally wounded at her feet, face down and
apparently immobile, although his right hand wouldn't seem
to die, and he sent the crowd into hysterics by hitting single,
dying notes every time she pronounced him dead and started
to walk away.

But Max was slow getting up after the lights went out,
unable to put any weight on his left hand, and when he staggered briefly from dizziness, Echo and Daniel helped him
offstage to the dressing room. "He'll never make it through
the second set," Daniel said. "What'd you do to yourself this
time?"

"I was in a car wreck," Max replied with uncharacteristic
directness. Echo sensed that, while Max pretty much flaunted
fucking up in other areas of his life, he didn't want Daniel
doubting his professionalism. "The doc injected my hand and
gave me some pills, but it's wearing off. I'll be okay if I can
ice it down. Have you got any blow?"

Daniel gave Echo an exaggerated eye-roll. He left the two
of them alone in the dressing room and went back to the bar
with the other band members to have a beer and pretend to
ignore fans.

Max went down the hall to get a bucket of ice while Echo
partially filled the washbasin with cold water for him. The
running water must have drowned out the sound of the door
opening and closing behind her; when she turned off the tap
and turned around, she saw Fishbone sitting backwards on a
folding chair.

He was dressed in a tight black suit, with an outdated
fedora, black shirt, and silver string tie. He smiled at her,
looking like a happy-face skeleton, and tipped the fedora.
"Howdy, Miss Echo. It's a real pleasure to see you again. And

hear you. You were terrific. If you don't mind my saying."

"Hey, Fish," Max said, coming through the door with the bucket of ice under his arm, as if seeing Z's hired killer in his dressing room were an expected and welcome sight.

"Max." Fish touched the brim of his hat again and looked at the ice bucket.

"Hurt my hand. Need to ice it down for the next set. You mind?" He walked over to the sink and dumped the ice into the water, incidentally putting himself between Echo and the killer. He rolled up the sleeve on his shirt and stuck his left hand into the frigid blend with a small gasp of pain as he talked. "So, you moving to a new crew out here, or what?"

"I'm still with Z."

"How's he doing?"

"Not well. That's why I'm here. He wants to see you."

"About what? If he wants the keys to his car back, I think LAPD has it in impound."

Echo watched Fish expectantly, to see if Max were pushing him the wrong way by reminding him that they'd had to flee for their lives the last time they'd seen Z. But Max had played it right. Fish smiled. "You know, I saw the two of you leaving L.T.'s with that car. I never told anyone."

Max took his hand out of the ice water, shook it briefly, and ran it over his face and through his hair. "Thanks. You didn't not kill us just so you can kill us now, did you? 'Cause you're not the sentimental type."

Fishbone laughed out loud this time. "Kid, I always liked you. Those other pretty boys were just Crisco with arms and legs, but you . . . And Echo here. How come she hasn't said hello or anything?"

"She can't talk anymore. Juno put a curse on her for helping Z."

Fishbone shrugged.

"She helped him, and then he told that fuck with the metal pecker to kill her. Kind of makes you wonder about the man, doesn't it, Fish?"

"No."

"Can I borrow your kit? I'm gonna need something to get me through the second set."

Fishbone pulled a large, compact black leather wallet from his jacket pocket and tossed it to Max, who unfolded it on the stand next to the sink. He drew out a hypodermic needle, a small spoon, and a glycine packet of white powder. While he worked, Echo edged as far from him as she could get.

"So tell me, Fish, why did Z send you all the way across the country? He could have called."

"He wanted to make sure you got the message. That you understood it was important."

"Okay, I got that."

"And he's not so far away anymore. We had to leave New Orleans."

Max finished tamping the powder into the spoon before he looked up. "What happened?"

"After Juno died, and the other witches, he had a run of bad luck. Unbelievable bad luck. He's in Vegas now."

"Hey, *we'll* be there in three days." Max didn't look over as he heated the underside of the spoon with his lighter. "You need tickets? I can comp you."

"Two days, actually, is when you get there. Z's waiting at the Luxor. You know, the casino that looks like a giant pyramid? I need to explain a few things to you first, about what's going down there."

Max was drawing the last of the heroin solution into the hypodermic when they all heard something outside the door. Before Max could move, Fish had leapt across the room, grabbed Echo, and pulled her into the bathroom, closing the door almost all the way behind them. Max stuffed the spoon and lighter into his pocket, but was still holding the hypodermic in his left hand when the door burst open. He jammed the hypo into the ice water and pretended surprise when he looked into the mirror over the sink and saw Nemo standing there, blocking the doorway and then some with his raincoated girth.

"Shit. Officer Nemo. Didn't we just do this?"

"I told you to stay away from him," Nemo growled, closing the door and advancing into the room, sweeping it with his eyes. "Where's the little girl?"

"Changing her diapers." Max nodded toward the bathroom. "And I did stay away from him."

"You were seen leaving the wreck this afternoon, Mr. Rock Star."

"How's he doing?"

Peering through the crack in the door with Fishbone at her side, Echo saw Nemo advance to within a foot of Max. "How d'ya think? When the hospital report showed he was drunk on duty when he ran his car into half the fuckin' street, he was suspended. Then he goes home, and tells his wife he's leaving her."

"Shit." Max's hand must have been starting to freeze up; Echo saw him take it out of the ice water briefly.

"And so she splits with this, uh, certain necklace he gave her, for which he could get in a lot of trouble."

"I'm sorry. Can I do anything?"

"You can die, is what you can do." Before Max could react, Nemo had him by the throat and was lifting him off the ground.

In a blur, Fishbone was through the bathroom door, knife in hand, heading straight for the big man's back.

Echo didn't scream. She couldn't have. But she must have

made some sort of sound, because Nemo turned in her direction just as Fishbone struck, turned just enough to throw off the killer's aim. Nemo roared with pain and let go of Max, turning on Fishbone, catching him with a backhand that bounced him off the near wall.

Ducking under the next swing, Fishbone came inside with the knife, stabbed Nemo in the lower chest. As Fish tried to withdraw the knife, it snagged in Nemo's raincoat, and the big man grabbed Fishbone's wrist, crushed it, slowly pried the knife from his fingers.

Max was pulling himself to his feet, trying to clear his head, when Fishbone yelled out. Nemo had the knife and was slashing wildly, opening huge gouges in Fishbone's arm and face.

Plunging his hand back into the basin, Max came out with the hypodermic and slammed it into the back of Nemo's neck just as Nemo jammed the knife into Fishbone's throat.

Blood fountained everywhere in slow and silent motion. The two struggling men slumped to the floor and lay still, while Max, panting and wild eyed, bent over the bodies.

Echo was still standing in the bathroom door, gaping, when Lucy walked in. Far less surprised at the tableau than one might expect, Lucy locked the door behind her, stepped around the bodies, and began to inspect Max, who was bleeding from the head and trying to get his breath back. "Are you all right?" she asked Echo, and when Echo nodded, she went back to Max. "I don't suppose you can play like this? Shit. Well, we'll just have to cancel the second set." She flipped a cell phone out of her handbag and punched in a number for the doctor. After a quick conversation, she phoned someone else, someone she called Roberto. Then Lucy approached the two bodies and gave each a tremendous kick in the groin with her pointed shoes. "Well, they must be dead," she said. "Now who's who here?"

Max explained as best as he could, while Echo wrapped some of the ice from the basin in a towel and applied it to the bruises on his neck.

"The killer saved you from the cop? That story will never sell. No, if this gets out, which I hope it doesn't, the cop tried to save you from the killer, and sacrificed his own life."

"But—"

"Trust me on this. Selling stories is my job. We get your fingerprints off the hypo—and, ah, anything else of the killer's you touched. Okay, what's in the syringe?"

"Heroin, I think," Max sighed.

"Heroin, *you think*?" Lucy gave him a troubled look. "You ought to know before using that shit, wouldn't you say? What if it were poison? Or too pure?"

He looked at her sheepishly.

She said, "If we need a story, that's how the killer was going to kill you, by making it look like an OD. Most of the heroin is still in the needle; Roberto probably can add a little something when he gets here."

"Roberto?"

"Don't ask. We have people to take care of this sort of thing." She shook her head. "Rock stars."

Lucy made another phone call, this one to someone inside the building, said she was kidnaping their act, apologized, said she'd make it up to them. Then she moved Max and Echo out of the dressing room, out the rear door, and into the back of a limo. "Now, why do you suppose this man tried to kill you?" she asked.

"He didn't. He was an old, ah, associate."

"Ah. Well, we'll play up the colorful bad boy angle." She got back on the cell phone, and soon a second stretch limo arrived, delivering Echo's and Max's suitcases.

"Uh, won't the cops want to talk to me? When a cop gets killed, they usually take it pretty personally, right?"

Lucy gave him The Look that said details are somebody else's business. "So, maybe you weren't here at all. Maybe the bodies aren't here. Let's let Roberto worry about that."

When the doctor arrived—the same doctor who had attended Max that afternoon—he joined them in the back seat. Besides tending to Max, he gave Echo a sedative. She settled back in the seat, and as their driver pulled out of the parking lot, she thought, *Just another day in LA.*

"At least somebody else is driving," Max yawned, as they headed out of town.

Echo wasn't listening. Feeling unreal and lightheaded, she closed her eyes and imagined the car floating up into the clouds.

Part III

Las Vegas

15

Not just another City Lite.
                    —Max

They rode across the desert, Echo and Max dozing on each other's shoulders, Lucy sitting in the seat opposite them, facing backwards toward LA, not yet finished with the place, punching numbers and talking quietly into her cell phone. Through veiled eyes, Echo watched Lucy frown as she hung up. Max must have seen the same thing, because Echo heard him ask quietly if something were wrong.

"Definitely," Lucy nodded. "I only have one more cell phone battery and another three hours of driving. We may have to make an emergency stop in Barstow, if I can locate an all-night Circuit City. Otherwise, America could be feeling something, and I wouldn't be the first to know it." She smiled faintly in her red power suit, allowing this irony to briefly crack all her hard angles and blond style.

Max said, "Tell me if I'm out of line for asking, Lucy, but do you ever have sexual feelings?"

Echo shut her eyes tight, but kept listening.

"Sure. My primary research center is south of the belly button."

"So, if you're hot for someone, you sign them up as a client?"

"You asking if I have sexual feelings about you? Sure, everybody does. That's why I like you."

"Because you do, or because everyone does?"

"The latter."

Max laughed quietly. "Everyone does want me. It makes it hard to trust people."

"You bet. That's why women like having a woman for an agent. If you think getting dumped by a lover hurts, wait'll you get screwed over by your agent."

"*You're* my agent."

"Hmmm."

"Ever get dumped by a lover?" Max asked.

Lucy's laugh was a verbal wince. "Only once, when I was at Berkeley. I lost it. I know, I know, hard to imagine, but I cried for a month. Almost flunked out, had an abortion. I hated losing control. Promised myself it would never happen again."

"So you became an agent."

She smiled.

"Think that would work for me?"

"No. I don't know what would, because I don't know what made you the way you are."

"Well, let's see, I'm from western New York originally, haven't been back since I left. Don't know if I'm still wanted for murder."

Echo found herself holding her breath as tightly as she was closing her eyes. She didn't want to think how little she knew of the man she loved, nor of the reasons she shouldn't love him, and he *couldn't* love her.

"I had parents who loved me, and they loved each other, too, but they hated at the same time. Always fighting, making up, fighting again. They'd get each other arrested for assault, and a week later they'd get busted for fucking in public. People told them to get divorced. I don't know why they didn't. They never said it was because of me.

"They drank a lot. Sometimes the alcohol made it a little better; usually it made it a lot worse. When I was ten, a social worker tried to take me away from them. They'd never hurt me or anything, but the court found them unfit. They told

me to pack a suitcase, and I wouldn't, so my dad packed it for
me, and then my mother unpacked it and packed it the way
she thought it should be. They started arguing about *that*.

"Then my dad took the suitcase and we all went and sat
outside, under a tree, smoking Marlboros. We had a swinging
bench that was big enough for the three of us, me being
pretty small at the time. It was a rural house, not a farm
house or anything, but pretty isolated, propane instead of
electricity. It was in a place called Arcadia. My mother said,
'If the house blew up or something, maybe we could all get
away and start over.'

"'Why blow up the house? Why not just leave?' my father
asked.

"My mother looked at him as if he were out of his mind.
'It's our house,' she said. 'We can't leave it.' And she went
back inside.

"We just sat there for a while, me and my father. Then my
father reached into his back pocket. He handed me all the
money in his wallet, and tossed it on the ground. I remember
thinking, it wasn't such a bad wallet, why the hell was he
throwing it away? Especially since he had his lighter in his
other hand, and he kept that. He gave me a big hug and told
me not to move. Then he went back inside.

"I didn't have to wait long. The house exploded about two
minutes later."

There was silence in the car for a moment, and then Lucy
started to laugh. "You son of a bitch. You had me going
there. I love the part about how they couldn't leave the
house, just like they couldn't leave each other. Nice touch."

Somewhere in there, Echo managed to drift off, remembering a cigar box containing Z's collection of mementos. In
it, he kept a red ribbon she'd worn around her ankle the first
night she sang in his club. There'd been an earring, a tar-

nished Zippo, some other, mostly worthless crap. And an old leather wallet.

"Either of you ever been to Vegas before?" the driver asked them.

Looking at the black man's face reflected in the rear view mirror reminded Echo of visiting her sister's old man in prison, having him talk through that tiny slit in the door because otherwise they'd have to talk over the phone and it might be recorded. This was like that, somehow, like she expected this stranger to give them crucial secret information. "If you haven't been here in the last couple years," he continued, "it's the same as never."

"Never," Max responded.

"Same thing." The man had golden eyes and a gold front tooth Echo saw when he smiled. "Practically none of the stuff you're gonna see on the Strip even existed a few years ago. See them dancing waters over there, in front of the Bellagio? They play some fake classical piece of shit—you guys don't play that shit, do you? Good—they play 'Singin' in the Rain' or something, and these fountains shoot up like trained cobras. Next door, the Mirage, that volcano's gonna erupt in ten minutes. Gotta be off the Strip by then, 'cause traffic locks up like a sonofabitch. Also, you occasionally get a Vietnam vet, upset about the napalm. Over there, Treasure Island, pirate attack just before dinner. Guys with swords in their teeth swing out right over the sidewalk. Fucking cannon ball almost took my head off once. Down there, you got the Excalibur, knights on horses jousting with lances, people paying fifty bucks to eat with their hands. See the Statue of Liberty over there, and the Eiffel Tower across the street?

"Ten years ago, this place was all about gambling. Don't get me wrong, it's still about gambling, but it's like now you got to hypnotize people with your special thang, so, when they lose, it's not like they're losing, it's like they're doing their thang."

"They're sacrificing to the designer god of their choice," Max suggested.

Everything the man said made perfect sense to Echo, because she could feel the different energies from each casino they passed. There was something intense, concentrated about the energies in this city that she'd never felt before. New Orleans had had three or four different energies, all ancient but distinct. LA had had a horrible, unrestrained, chaotic force she'd been glad to leave behind. In Las Vegas, she was feeling a dozen or more rivers of force, not united exactly, but somehow woven together, so that a bit of one would vibe to her here, and again, more briefly perhaps, a few blocks later, only to disappear as swiftly as it had come. Was there a pattern? Probably, one that would emerge if she were patient and lucky. Or unlucky, she realized, because, like Juno had said, reading the forces was one thing, doing anything with them was an entirely different matter.

"That pyramid job, over there," Max asked, "is that the Luxor?"

"Yeah, but don't ask me what the name has to do with mummies and that shit."

"Luxor is the same as Thebes," Max said. "City on the Nile where the pharaohs had a big-ass temple."

Echo smiled and elbowed him.

"Don't give me that look. I don't spend *all* my time shooting drugs and screwing. Remember that time you caught me reading a comic book? Besides, Terry told me."

Echo was trying to get a better look at the casino, a better feel, but she was too far away to sense anything but a faint eeriness.

As they were turning off the Strip, Max asked, "What's that new one, that big thing they're building down there at the end?"

"Oz," the driver told them. "The biggest and the best. Course, they all say that when they're building them."

The car pulled in front of the Hard Rock Hotel. Except for the trademark giant guitar, the place was unspectacular after the otherworldly visions of the Strip. It even had spider web-thin cracks in the masonry arches in the lobby, as if the place had been built by one of Z's union crews. Rock and roll, Max once said, is planned obsolescence with a back beat.

The lobby reminded Echo of the back lot at Universal Studios, a bunch of props waiting for a plot to happen. A full-sized pink Cadillac was on display next to an enormous slot machine. If you dropped in a five dollar token and three Elvises came up, you won the car. Enormous crystal chandeliers hung overhead, and clothing, framed record albums, and guitars lined the walls. Echo had never been in any hotel lobby before, not counting the Olympus Motor Inn back in Athens, but this was pretty much how she imagined they all looked.

The reservations desk was manned by beautiful young women made up to look like famous people: Madonna, Cher, Crissy Hate.

"Next time you're here," Lucy told Echo, "they'll be made up to look like *you*." She picked up their keys—which weren't keys at all, but plastic cards with holes punched in them—at the front desk, and told Echo and Max where their rooms were. *Rooms*. They were in separate rooms. Echo frowned.

Bellhops, dressed like regular bellhops, took their bags and led them into the elevators. Echo didn't like having someone else carry her stuff, it just didn't seem right, but it did leave her hands free so she could hang onto Max's arm—until they reached the ninth floor, where Max stepped off. Why would they put her on ten and Max on nine? Was this Lucy's doing?

"It's okay," Max assured her. "I'll meet you in the lobby in an hour. I wanna be there for Inner War's sound check."

He blew her a kiss, but the door slid shut on it; snatched it from her in the moment before she would possess it.

16

You are what's left after you've been eaten.
                                                    —Max

Drugged and semi-beaten, Max had slept most of the way to Vegas, so when the bellhop opened his door, he was in too big a hurry to piss to even look around. Still, when he'd washed his hands and re-entered the room, he was surprised to find he could have missed anything the size of Truck Stop.

"Don't worry about the tip," the big man said. "I told the kid I was from the union."

"Bet he didn't even ask to see your card," Max smiled. Then he frowned. "Fish is dead."

Truck was motionless, in shock.

"A cop did it. They'll probably say he was trying to kill me, and the cop tried to stop him. But it was the other way around. I got the cop."

"You got the cop?"

Max held up his injured hand. "Fish opened him up, and I finished him. But it was too late." Where Truck Stop was concerned, things were best kept simple, with plenty of visual aids.

Truck reflected a moment, then nodded. "It's better you tell it the first way. Professional pride, you know."

Max relaxed. "You're here for Z, right?"

"He wants to see you Aesop."

"You mean ASAP?"

"Right now."

The walk to the Luxor took no more than fifteen minutes, but both men were sweating profusely by the time they entered the lobby of the huge glass pyramid and proceeded on into the actual casino and hotel behind it. The place smelled of Clorox, and Max guessed they'd been having problems with the fake Nile River that meandered through the ground floor. Truck confirmed that people had a tendency to pour their warm cocktails into it, and occasional cigarette butts and the odd keno card. He also said that a gondolier, or whatever you called the Egyptian version piloting Cleopatra's Barge, had gone missing in the middle of his shift last week. Truck was professionally interested in this last. "Not even that fuckin' David Copperfield can make a stiff disappear into three feet of water." He was also very enthusiastic about the virtual reality ride, which he said sounded like his favorite video game, Tomb Raider. You got into a seat surrounded by an IMAX-sized movie screen, and it felt first as if you were plummeting down an elevator to an underground mine, then speeding along rickety rails in an out-of-control coal cart. Truck thought it could be improved if the passengers were given automatic weapons.

Truck's thinking was childish, but not stupid, and it was this childishness, Max thought, that explained the man's loyalty to his boss, the loyalty of a son to a father. Even though the father is a cold-blooded killer.

They entered an elevator that sagged slightly under Truck's weight, and started up. "Before the cop interrupted us," Max remembered, "Fish said he had some important stuff to tell me before the meeting with Z."

Truck looked at him. "Like what?"

"I thought you might know."

Truck reflected, and as the door to the penthouse slid open, he said, "Well, maybe it was the disease."

The window at the other end of the suite looked down on the Pyramid. Max could make out the Oz construction project in the distance. A large armchair had been turned to face it, and Max could see, in the chair, an elderly man hooked to an IV rig. Against all evidence to the contrary, Truck Stop was addressing that chair as if it contained Z.

"Boss," he bellowed for the third or fourth time, grimacing briefly at Max. Finally a frail hand lifted from the chair and waved for Max or Truck Stop or both to take a chair off to the side of the big picture window.

Z's mountainous frame was not just shrunken from some wasting disease, it was twisted and shriveled and blotched with purple and brown welts. One of his ears was bandaged over, perhaps missing, which, Max supposed might have accounted for his inability to hear Truck Stop. The head turned briefly toward Max, but thick dark glasses hid the man's eyes.

"Hey, kid."

"Z. Is that really you? Or are you fucking with me?"

"I was fucking with you when I gave you that gun and sent you to Juno's."

"I wondered about that."

"Nothing personal. Didn't particularly want you dead, but I couldn't get myself to do her. I was making a half-assed gesture, figuring you still had a chance in a million of getting out of there when the shooting started. You follow me?"

Max didn't, but shrugged. For one thing, it didn't explain why he'd sent Echo, an asset of some value, back there to be killed as well.

"From that moment of indecision, of weakness . . . " He gestured vaguely at his own ruined body.

"So, you lost that war?"

"Hell no. Well, not in the guns and dollars sense. I'm a well-respected man, at least by those who haven't seen me since. But Juno got even. Right before the end, she must have figured out I'd gotten the charm of her youth away from Greta. Probably got it out of your little friend, Echo. And somehow she did this to me before she died. Or maybe after. Who the hell knows?"

"You killed Greta?"

"And burned Juno's house. Thought there might be stuff in there I wouldn't want to see some dark night. She'd trained those little shadow shits to get into your ears and eyes and make you see and hear and feel shit. Spiced up the sex, I can tell you, but I didn't know what else they could do. Anyway, no one seems to be able to do much for me."

"Tough luck."

Z swivelled his head a bit in Max's direction, and something that looked like a smile crept across his face. "Give the kid a beer," he said over his shoulder.

Truck opened a full-sized refrigerator, not one of those dinky hotel jobs, and brought Max a Dixie. "Imported from your old home town," Z boasted.

Max took a sip, and waited, and finally said, "So you think *I* can do something about this?"

"Maybe." Z returned his black gaze to the window. "Maybe not. See that casino they're building over there?"

"Oz?" Z tensed at the name, and Max added, "The limo driver said that's what it was called, that's all."

"You know how we ran construction back in Orleans? Well, out here, everything is unionized, and certain interests control all the unions. Business is booming, which is good for those interests. Then some weird shit starts to happen on this new construction project. The people running this town are pros. But this weird shit they've never seen before."

"You're talking about magic?"

Z's feeble head nodded slightly. The folds of flesh on his chicken neck wobbled. "So someone decides to call me.

Apparently I got a reputation for dealing with the weird shit. You follow me so far?"

"Go on."

"A few months ago, when I was invited out here, I'm already a bit peaked, see, but as far as these guys know, I've taken over all of Orleans, which everybody else always stayed away from because of the magic. And I'm not shy, so I come out and take a look. But the first time I step onto that site, I practically collapse. I get myself back here, but I still get worse, way worse, every fucking day. So now I got two things on my mind."

"One is, you think there's something on that site that's connected to the old magic? Juno's magic?"

"He's smart," Z said over his shoulder. "I keep forgetting Fish ain't with me any more. What's this bullshit about him trying to kill you?"

"He saved my ass," Max said. "He walked in on a situation and got killed trying to protect me."

"Trying to protect *me*," Z snorted. "He knew I needed to see you."

"You were saying there were *two* things on your mind."

"The second . . . " Z made a feeble gesture of dismissal. "The second is that I can't let anybody see me like this before I get the first part figured out. Those 'interests' I was mentioning, they don't have no use for someone who fucks up. So it's important I get this business straightened out in a hurry."

"Meaning . . . you need a witch, fast."

Z nodded. "Your little friend, Echo, she's got some ability."

"And you didn't kidnap *her*, because . . . ?"

"Let's say I learned my lesson. I figure being ugly with Juno got me bad, and coming onto that construction site with her mark on me and evil thoughts on my mind made it a whole lot worse. But you can control Echo. She's in love with you."

"She doesn't have the kind of control Juno had." Max stopped short of telling Z that Echo had been cursed as well and couldn't do a thing about it; what would Z do if he thought Echo couldn't deliver? "But, well, I guess it wouldn't hurt to ask her." *As long as I don't expect an answer*, he thought. "I can see what she knows, anyway."

"That's my boy. And, kid, maybe it's better you don't tell her this is to help me? She might, you know . . . "

"Bear a grudge for your murdering someone she loved and letting your henchman try to rape and kill her?"

"Don't get technical."

Z's voice was sharp; Max backed off. "I'll get on it. We have a rehearsal in a few minutes and a show tonight, but first thing in the morning. You have a phone number here you trust?"

Z shook his head. "My employers control the phones. This room's not bugged, but if you call, make the message kind of general, okay?"

That's useful information if I want you off my back, Max thought. *The disease is killing your mind, too. Unless, of course, the phone's not bugged and it's another way to test my loyalty. You always were big on tests.*

Z gave him a card, said he was supposed to show it to anybody on the site who questioned his presence. It listed Z as a consultant to the construction company.

As he turned to go, Max saw the old cowboy boots, up against the wall next to the closet, and he couldn't figure out for some time why the sight bugged him the way it did.

There was something about this elevator—this building?

this town?—that made Echo feel as if she'd stepped into the mouth of an enormous beast and it was tasting her, deciding whether to spit her out or swallow.

She felt the floor drop away from her, clung to it only by imagining the soles of her shoes were sticky with magic. Didn't you have to press one of the buttons before it just took off like this? The hair on her scalp rose. Why couldn't Max have come up to her room for her? If only she'd been able to ask. If only he'd been able to hear.

She watched the numbers on the control panel briefly illuminate as she descended. It was like a rocket ship count-down that wouldn't stop at zero, because there *was* no zero. Three . . . two . . . L. That must be one—but the elevator didn't stop, it went lower. There was another pause when it finally did stop, and then, as she reached forward with one tentative hand to push, the doors slid open. There was no pink Cadillac, no reservation desk.

She could still feel the giant mouth of the elevator breath-ing moistly around her as she stepped forward into a space defined only by the light coming from the open door. The floor should have been concrete, or carpet, but was complete-ly covered by and laced with rope-like coils of a material that seemed both clay and metal at the same time. While she was trying to get her balance on the inch-high ridges, the elevator doors closed behind her and she was left in darkness.

She reached a hand in front of her, took a step forward, and then another, and immediately came in contact with a wall that felt much like the floor beneath her feet. She was wondering why, if it had been so close, she hadn't seen it from the elevator. One of the coils seemed to move beneath her hand, then came to rest again. Perhaps her natural im-pulse should have been to jerk her hand away, but the tactile experience was less like a slithering snake than a cat rearranging itself beneath a petting hand. Echo trusted her feelings and left her hand where it was.

Hello, something didn't say.

It wasn't her imagination, because she was able to say "Hello" back. She put both hands on the pythonesque section of the thing lining the wall, felt it swell appreciatively under her touch. Then the entire basement began to glow faintly, illuminated by a chaos of rainbow phosphorescence that ran in thin ribs along the creature's tendrilled body, which made up the entire wall, the wall in front of her, as far as she could see. She gasped with pleasure, and understood something of the thing's immensity as it curved out of her sight in the distance, and literally disappeared into the floor at her feet. Disappeared: it did not begin or end there, but simply vanished from sight. Like the substantial fog she had seen in the after-hours shack in New Orleans, it did not fit wholly into this world, but somehow overlapped with it.

Echo sang to it, but she avoided "Voodoo Magic."

It was too damn hot out as Max walked back to the Hard Rock Hotel, but there was plenty to look at. An enormous roller coaster was running across the skyline of New York City, and patrons were screaming, as they always seemed to. On the other side of the Strip, behind the MGM, a single individual strung on gigantic bungee cords rocketing between two towers. A volcano erupted further up the street. These people don't know shit about thrills, Max thought.

He wasn't surprised Echo was no longer waiting for him in the lobby. He called her room on a house phone, and when she didn't answer, he headed for the concert arena, knowing that would be the biggest attraction for her.

He showed the crew bouncer at the door an ID Lucy had given him. Inner War was up on stage, doing a sound check.

Crissy Hate herself, the razor-thin rocker Max had admired for years, was in a shitty mood, because no one could fix her damn mike. The band played a couple chords, and the weirdest feedback Max had ever heard crawled out of the amps, a sort of low keening sound, like a lonesome whale on K. Crissy shouted into the mike, over the noise, just to make her point. "Look, I don't want to break balls here, but don't tell me you alleged Hard Rock fuckers don't even have a sound man that can fix your own system! What about you?" Like everyone else he'd ever met, Crissy Hate, winner of four Grammys and widow of two rock and roll husbands, had her attention immediately drawn to Max.

Caught off guard, Max did one of those Who? Me? things. When he realized she'd mistaken him for a grip, he shrugged compliance, though he had no clue what he might do that hadn't already been done. Her guys must have already checked their leads, and the few sound boards he'd worked with in New Orleans were far less sophisticated than what they had here. As he was about to move to the stage, the door he'd just come through opened again, and Echo appeared. She was flushed and excited, and ran into his arms before he could turn away.

"All you need is love," Crissy sighed over the whale screech. "But Hate needs a sound check."

At the sound of the electronic keening, Echo appeared startled, and then excited again. Drawing Max by the hand, she took him up on stage, over to the microphone Crissy had taken to whipping with a feather boa. Max went to check the guitar leads, which looked fine to him, but Echo went up to the mike and started humming into it. She was singing back the whale-like sounds the system had been emitting every time someone spoke into it. A minute later, she was deeply into an a capella solo, and the keening sound had changed tone and was fading. Another minute, and the noise was gone, and Echo sang out, "I'm the girl of your dreams, long black whip and studded jeans," in perfect imitation of Crissy Hate's own performance of "Male Parts," on the *To Die For* CD. The band picked it up, and played through the entire song with her. Crissy laughed with pleasure.

17

We are our paths' destinations.
            —Max

The red silk wallpaper crawling with golden, flame-breathing dragons looked understated, here in Vegas. They were having Chinese food with Inner War, and Crissy Hate was trying to explain what had happened with her sound check, but when she looked to Echo for help, Echo could only look to Max. The two of them had been huddled together through much of dinner, trying to sort things out through sign language, intuition, and brief written messages. It was clear to Echo that the sound check and what she'd encountered in the basement of the hotel were connected, but she had no idea how Max was going to explain it to strangers.

"Well, Echo has kind of a way with sounds," he said finally.

"Yeah, like Einstein had a way with numbers," Crissy laughed.

Echo shivered, reminded of the $E^2=MC$ she'd seen scrawled on so many walls back in Echo Park: Ecstasy Squared equals MindCum, someone had translated it.

"I guess she just fed back the feedback until it sorted itself out," Max concluded lamely, probably hoping there were no engineers in the crowd.

Echo thought, Well, that makes as much sense as telling them I met an electric super creature in a lower level basement (a level there's not even a button for on the elevator panel), a creature with some sort of consciousness, definitely not a human consciousness, and that my intuitive communications with it *did* basically amount to feeding back to it a version of the vibrations it put out.

She had been staring at the wallpaper above their table while she ruminated, and was sure the dragons had been crawling and tossing their heads, until she refocused on them.

Later that evening, as they rode along the Strip back to the Hard Rock Hotel, Crissy was telling Echo about a therapist she knew who might be able to help her with her speech problem. "Don't give up just because you went to one high-priced Beverly Hills shrink for a couple weeks. Lucy sent you, right? You can't fucking trust anyone Lucy sent you to. Your agent is not your friend, girl. She doesn't want to rock the boat. What if she sent you to a therapist who cured your speaking problem but you lost your singing voice? See what I mean?"

They stopped the limo to watch the volcano erupt in front of the Mirage. The spectacular explosion drew appreciative exclamations from the crowds, but again Echo was overcome with a sense of dread.

As the orange-red of the eruption faded from the night, and the limo began to pull away, there was another enormous squeal of delight from the crowd on the street, and Echo again pressed her face to the window. "Hel—lo," Crissy said, and she stood up on the back seat with her head out the moonroof. Echo's eyes widened, and then she was standing up next to Crissy to get a better view.

The lurid marquees of every hotel on the Strip were so spectacular and exotic, each in its own way, that it took Echo a moment to realize what she was seeing. Instead of flashing and dancing in their own rhythms, every electric light on the Strip seemed to have synchronized, sometimes pulsing in a single rhythm, sometimes playing a counter-point to each other. It was as if the casinos were talking together, Echo thought, as if they were all part of one giant beast.

Only when individual light bulbs and neon tubes began to explode did the crowd begin to panic. As glass rained down, Echo dragged Crissy back inside the limo so the driver could close the moonroof. Some glass got in, littering the limo floor. And Echo saw, lying among the shards, a single casino chip. She picked it up; it was a $500 chip from Oz. On its face, the Wicked Witch of the West winked at Echo.

"Tell me this has happened before," Max said.

"Must be a promotion," Crissy shrugged.

"For what? The Apocalypse?"

Next morning, Echo found Max sitting at her breakfast table with a pot of coffee, looking through a local newspaper. "A bunch of stuff about the lights on the Strip last night," he said. "It wasn't planned, or at least no one is taking the blame for it. There was a ton of damage. The crews are already out there," he gestured toward the window, "trying to get the marquees up and running again. Good thing 'Echo and Narcissus' was only up in black letters, huh?"

Echo sat up in bed and looked out the window. "Bunch of people caught the whole thing on their video cams," Max told her. "Encryption experts are claiming there was a definite pattern to the lights, like they were signaling bombers or something, except no one can figure out who'd want to bomb Las Vegas. Flying saucer people are having a field day. This one mathematician says it was definitely a chaos pattern, with that new Oz project as the 'strange attractor,' whatever that means." He looked closely at Echo, his grin gone. "I thought I'd tell you that, since we're supposed to go over there this morning."

Echo shivered.

"I don't blame you for not wanting to mess with this. Especially with Z involved. But I was thinking, what's his scam this time? He's going to die unless he can reverse Juno's curse, and he thinks Oz has something to do with that curse, says it accelerated his decay. So maybe he's figuring you can make Oz reverse his curse or something, I don't know. Of course then I was also thinking, why the hell should we help Z? Motherfucker tried to kill us once and might again, and we'd never even know why. Then I thought, if it could end Z's curse, it could end ours. Yours and mine, Echo."

Tears welled up in her eyes. He held her, and she wept like a baby, because it was the closest he'd ever come to saying he wished he could love her.

They took a cab to the Oz construction site, only to find the entire block fenced off, with construction warning signs posted everywhere. They stood at what Echo assumed would be the front entrance to the enormous casino: a yellow brick road, dusted with just a subliminal hint of Vegas gold, stretching away from them toward the gates of an Emerald City that should have made the MGM Grand cringe like a cowardly lion. A rickety-looking farm house, perhaps designed to spin on one corner, lay collapsed and inert off to the right of the entrance. There was not a munchkin in sight.

Something hung over the place, Echo knew, something there and not there, the shadow of a cloud, when there wasn't a cloud in the sky.

She could see that Max was about to forget he was a pampered rock star and jump the fence, when they both spotted a security man in a yellow hard hat who was in the act of spotting them. He was slight and a bit bent, and Echo studied him as he drew closer, studied him because she felt just a touch of strangeness coming from him.

"Sorry," he said, "this site ain't open to tourists."

"Someone asked us to check it out," Max told him.

"Lots of people come by here to check it out. Want to take each other's pictures with the Scarecrow, that kind of shit. But it's a dangerous place, and nobody's allowed in."

"I know construction sites are dangerous," Max persisted, "but we were sent over here by, well, one of the foremen." He held out the card Z had given him.

"I wasn't talking about the hazards of construction," the little man said as he read the card. "What are you kids, some-body's niece or nephew or something?"

Max thought about it a moment. "Well, in a way."

Echo couldn't decide whether to warn him off. The little man didn't seem dangerous, just strange, thin in some way other than the obvious, almost as if he were an image projected on a screen. But Max didn't seem to notice that.

"Take a tip from me, sonny. If your Godfather's sending you over here, he don't care much for your side of the family."

"We were sent here because of the weird stuff that's sup-posedly been happening."

"The weird stuff." The man wasn't asking a question.

"Yeah. We're—well, *she's* kind of a specialist in weird stuff."

The old man's eyes were distant for a moment. "Have you seen the dragon?"

Echo shook her head.

The man looked at her solemnly for a moment. Echo could tell he liked her, or something about her. "Well you should see . . . something . . . before I let you in there. And understand, I'm still not going with you. Come on. It's over in my cabin."

They followed him around the block to a construction trailer, up the wooden steps into the one-room living quarters and office. At one end was a bank of security cameras showing the sides of the lot, which explained how he'd become aware of their presence so quickly. The man popped a video cassette into a player. "Nobody knows I got it, and I don't suppose anybody cares either, but don't feel obligated to spread the word. Your . . . relative probably wouldn't like it if this leaked out to the press."

The screen showed Oz, much as it now looked, in a night view lit by dozens of huge arc lamps. Men were fleeing the site, big men, a lot of them, running right toward and past the camera. The camera started to shake and the lights started to fall, and at first Echo thought it was an earthquake, because the ground behind the men suddenly seemed to be rising and falling, roiling in huge, ridged mounds. But she realized almost immediately what it was she was seeing. Why are you running? she wanted to shout. It's only reacting to your fear; it didn't hurt *me!*

The tape ended, and the old man said, "Next morning, a S.W.A.T. team went in and hauled out some of the bodies. They didn't see any trace of a half-dozen missing guys. The ones they *could* find were missing pieces. Not chewed off, just missing, like these guys had been born without legs or arms or heads, except we'd all seen 'em wearing them the day before."

Echo shuddered.

"Oh, that ain't the worst part. When the Union sent in its own investigators that night, they were attacked by what they thought were the characters in the Oz story. A lion. A scarecrow. An iron man."

"Tin man," Max corrected.

"Whatever. What they saw in there, before that happened, was weird, too. Changes in the architecture. And the wiring. Stuff had been reconnected and moved around in ways that made no sense."

"Like things seemed to have only two dimensions?" Max asked him. "Or too *many* dimensions?"

"What? I don't know. Maybe. That something I missed in *The Wizard of Oz*? I only saw the movie. But like I said, that wasn't the worst part."

The little man slumped back in his chair. Echo could somehow feel it pressing into his back, not just against it, but into it, as if the chair and the man were superimposed three-dimensional images. "I went to see some of the boys that made it out alive. They ain't all there anymore. I don't mean just mentally. You look at their faces from one angle, and they seem okay, and then from another angle, you can't see 'em at all. Then they turn back toward you, and you swear they have two noses or only one giant eye. Rumor is, they don't have heartbeats, and instead of moving blood they have this yellow, blue, or green neon that pulses in their veins. But I only heard that, I ain't seen it." There were tears in his eyes now. "One guy, Bert Russell, was my best friend. I go to see Bert, and he can't even talk." He looked at Echo, and she wondered if he somehow sensed her condition. "But the worst part is, he keeps reaching out, like he's trying to touch something, and I can see his hand disappear and come back again. And then, one time—he knows I'm there this time—he pulls me over and he's all excited, and he reaches out, and his hand disappears, and it comes back again. And he opens the hand to show me what he's got in it, and I can see there's a hole right through his hand. Not bleeding or anything, just a hole. But when you look into it, you don't see blood and bone, and you don't see what's on the other side of it, you see this blackness, blackness with something moving inside of it."

The little man stopped talking. He wasn't looking at them anymore. Or at least he wasn't seeing them.

* * *

"Okay," Max said when they were back out on the street and walking swiftly away from Oz, "let's rethink this before we just march in there. You're sure this thing likes you?"

Echo looked at him.

"Well, maybe it loses its powers during the daytime. It didn't attack the S.W.A.T. team. So it's afraid of sunlight? It's a vampire dragon!"

Echo made a face and shook her head.

"This whole town's asleep during the day, why shouldn't this thing be asleep too?"

To his astonishment, Echo looked at him less skeptically this time.

"What? I was kidding. It gambles? It goes to shows?"

She inhaled deeply, adding an expansive arm gesture.

"It breathes? What? The electricity? But they use a lot during the day, too, with all the air conditioning cranked up. Where's a pen and paper when you need 'em?"

She pointed to groups of people outside casinos.

"The people? It breathes people's . . . energies?" He watched Echo run through a series of faces. "Emotions? Our feelings?" She gave him one last look. "Our passions?"

She bit her lower lip and stared at him. She could tell he wanted to kiss her, he really did. "*That's* why it reacts to your singing. You convey exactly what it's looking for."

He held her for a while, somewhere between the Statue of Liberty and the Eiffel Tower, and let Oz be far away.

18

Once Max figured out who he was, everything else bored him. The band, Narc, was boring, despite its success. The groupies were très boring. Even his own yet-undiscovered lyrics had, to him, a predictability, like the running figures on a Grecian urn turned once too often in his hands.

—Perry White, *Memories of Max*

"We went there," Max said, "but when we heard some of the stuff that happened there, we realized we were underprepared."

Z stared at him through sunglasses. It was late in the day, Max's break between rehearsal and their eight o'clock opening. He should have been eating with Echo and the band, but if he was going to visit Z alone, he wanted it to be when he was shortly expected somewhere else, so he'd be missed if he didn't show up. Z looked out the window, toward Oz. "I told you it was a magic problem."

"Yeah, but you forgot to mention the murder and mayhem and missing heads. That's usually your favorite part."

"I haven't been myself lately."

Max looked again at the cowboy boots resting next to the closet. Were they slightly singed? "Someone mentioned a dragon."

Z shrugged. "Bullshit rumors. That's all. What's in Oz ain't a dragon."

"You know this thing, whatever it is, isn't just at Oz. Your little fence isn't exactly the DMZ."

Z nodded. "Concrete is cracking all over town, buildings are settling. Lights and electrical systems are acting funny.

One guy wins at video poker, and suddenly everybody else at the bar is hitting the jackpot, like a chain reaction. It's not supposed to happen that way, you know? You drop a gold nugget here or there so the rest of the suckers swarm in and get taken. A lot of the casinos are shutting down the video stuff entirely. Which translates into a few bucks. If you can get this solved, people would be very appreciative."

Right, thought Max. The Nevada Gaming Commission is relying on a couple of teenage musicians who happened to see *Ghostbusters* on cable. What the hell was Z really after? "So what is it you want us to do? Play it a hand of poker? We win and it leaves town? It wins and . . . " He got up to stretch his legs. Truck watched him with one eye from the bed, the other eye on the sports book scrolling down the TV's gaming channel.

"Find out what it wants. Find out what it's doing in there. Find out what it can do for us. The first step in taking over a territory from somebody stronger than you is to make a deal where you get something in return for not doing something you don't want to do anyway."

Max picked up one of the cowboy boots and looked at the bottom. A perfectly round hole the size of a casino chip was burned right through the sole. *You already know what it can do for you, but you're not telling me*, Max thought. *Why? Because it might be even more willing to do the same for us?* "So what can you offer it?"

Z nodded. "We know it's building something in there. Rebuilding. Maybe it wants to finish the casino in its own special way, a way that wouldn't necessarily interfere with running the casino. Put the boot down. It's . . . filthy."

"You're gonna make a monster a silent partner in the casino?"

"I've always been flexible."

"Hey, it could work. Maybe it'll only eat low rollers. Or big winners. Mind if I wash my hands before I head back? I have a show to do. We'll go back over there tomorrow and see if Echo can establish contact." *Hopefully the kind where we don't get killed.*

"It's just like singing in a bar," Max told Echo before their first big entrance onto the stage at the Hard Rock.

"Right," Daniel whined nervously. "Except it's not a bar, the sound system is totally whacked, and we're opening for a famous ball buster who's not gonna like it if we suck, and is gonna hate it if we're great. Plus, the crowd paid forty bucks a seat to see Inner War, and the management just wants us to do our set and get the hell off, so people will go back to gambling."

"Shit, you're right," Max snorted. "We'd better open with a song about Siegfried and Roy."

"Singing in a bar," Echo repeated, seemingly preoccupied, but she gave Max an idea. He walked out onto the stage while the roadies were still fiddling with the setup, picked up a guitar, started to tune it. Echo caught on and came out to adjust the height of the mike, check her amp, just another roadie herself. Hey, no one in this crowd had seen either of them before, except maybe in clothing ads. Daniel suddenly remembered what Max had done the first night they played together in LA. He whispered instructions to the keyboard and bass players, then slumped out on stage himself to begin readjusting his drum kit.

The crowd was still filing in, studying ticket stubs, complaining about the quality of seats, talking loudly about winning and losing and the buffet.

Max's tuning became slightly more noticeable than the other roadie noises, and after a moment, when it became apparent that he was using a couple strings to make the chiming sounds the casinos all used to announce that it was almost show time, there was a smattering of laughter. In the meantime, Echo was humming into her mike, eliciting horrendous feedback sounds, sounds that became the keening noises that had been troubling bands all week. There were groans from those who had heard about the problem. But Echo sang back to it, moving her arms and shoulders like she was a whale or a dolphin, and people started to look. And she went on, alone, gaining volume and melody with the noises, until the keening subsided and she was suddenly alone, scatting in full voice in a terrific solo that silenced pretty much the entire audience, even those who still couldn't decide if this was the show or just a talented roadie fooling around. Daniel—who had seated himself discretely behind his drums—and Max began playing a subdued counterpoint, merely a note here and there, behind Echo.

When Echo finished, the only sound in the auditorium was a subsonic pulsing that seemed to come from everywhere and nowhere. Max ripped into an electric guitar riff he'd spun off Echo's solo, and Daniel came in at almost the same time. A moment later, when the bass player, who'd started offstage, and the keyboard player joined them, the audience was roaring with approval, and someone finally had the presence of mind to turn down the house lights. They'd just done something no one else ever had in the history of rock and roll. They'd started ten minutes early.

After the show and the party and Lucy's scolding because they hadn't worn GrungeWear, Echo and Max took a cab back toward the Oz site, assuring the cab driver they had no intention of getting out.

Max reported his conversation with Z, and added his

suspicions. The boots in particular bothered him, although he couldn't explain why. "I mean, in a way it makes sense. He never took those boots off, and now, even when they're wrecked, he doesn't want to throw them out or let anyone touch them. But he said they were 'filthy.' I never heard him use that word before. This is a guy who would eat pizza that fell on the street upside-down and got run over by a garbage truck. And I snuck a look in the medicine cabinet. There are a whole bunch of little colored bottles in there with no labels, just different shapes and sizes, and dried herbs, not from the store, the kind Juno used to have hanging all over her house."

"Juno," Echo said suddenly, sitting up straight in her seat.

"The last time we saw her, she was stone cold dead." Max blinked. "Besides, there was no lady's shaving crap or Tampax or anything in Z's bathroom. She's not alive."

But Echo's look was less than reassuring. She tapped the cab driver on the shoulder and pointed across the street from the Oz block.

"What? You said you weren't gettin' out," the cab driver reminded them. "This is not a safe place."

"She just wants to look," Max assured him absently. Then he reflected, "He never took off the boots, except when he was in Juno's house."

Echo opened the cab door and stepped out onto the sidewalk. Max followed.

"Don't you two think about walking off without paying me," the driver said. "I know where you live."

There was no other traffic around. Max was vaguely aware of the cab driver complaining behind him as Echo stood in the middle of the street and lifted her arms and began to sing.

This time, there was nothing so obvious as the keening they had heard back at the auditorium, no electric sound system to serve as interface. But the casino itself, Max thought, seemed to be attending her. He was pretty sure the street was vibrating under his feet. The pavement—no, the air itself—began a gentle pitch and roll. Echo was calling it out, calling it up.

"Don't do that!" the cab driver yelled.

The little watchman they had met earlier came loping around the corner in a crippled run, faltered, went down on all fours, but then rose and continued running toward them.

And then they saw it. It had to be what the watchman had called the "dragon."

Max had only seen photos of the aurora borealis, the brilliant waves of solar radiation that the next day's newspapers claimed had suddenly appeared over the Nevada desert, but he thought "dragon" was a better description for this. The waves of colored energy rose in swirling trails from all over the casino grounds, and, like smoke in reverse, narrowed and concentrated themselves as they drifted skyward. Red, green, blue, yellow, orange, and a half-dozen trace colors coalesced three hundred feet in the air into something the size of an airplane. It looked scaled one moment, feathered the next, somewhere between substantial and insubstantial, an image, a reflection of something very real that existed just around the corner, just out of human sight. And then, as it shifted around itself in the sky, it opened one enormous eye in the middle of its forehead. And looked directly at Echo.

Fire—could it have been fire? No, there was no heat, more a stream of cold electrical energy in the air, red, golden, roaring down toward Echo. Max stepped forward to protect her, only to be thrown back as it slammed into the pavement between them.

When he looked up from the ground, he saw Echo, untouched, her arms raised to the sky, surrounded by a wall of this strange cold flame, still singing, and the air all around ringing with a responding energy.

He never heard the cab speed off, though he was vaguely aware of the sickening crunch it made as it ran over the little watchman.

19

This story is a tapestry, pegged across a stone wall between birth and death, covering a hole through which life escaped.
— Perry White, *Memories of Max*

Echo gazed out her window at Oz, still shadowed, even in daylight, by the outlines of strange energies. *It's strange you have this gift you only use to sing in bars.* Well, Juno, I'm not just singing in bars anymore.

Her moments in the circle of energy already seemed like a dream, a dream that expanded every time she looked at it, until she was unsure now if the dreams she'd had all night were recollections of that moment, or the fruit of dream-seeds planted by the dragon thing.

Its dragon-like appearance even arose in her dreams. The thing had her dreaming of dinosaurs! Dinosaurs fighting, and chasing, eating, giving birth, mating—the last of which was not easy to handle, perhaps because it reminded her of Z.

The irony of being unable to speak and yet expected to explain the impossible did not escape her as she sat with Max over coffee.

"Okay, I didn't get the sense it was looking for more copper wiring or cinder blocks for whatever it's building. But you think it wants . . . *dinosaurs?*"

Echo shook her head. It didn't *want* them exactly. The thing had appeared in a dinosaur-like form, she realized, because it had *expected* dinosaurs. It was as if it were looking for the dinosaurs, or remembered them, and thought Echo might too, and so left the vision, as a sign on a lamppost, *Have You Seen My Dog?*

*   *   *

They waited outside Z's hotel room at the Luxor until the
bogus message Max had left for Truck Stop from a "construction consultant" lured the large man to leave his employer's side. As the elevator groaned away with Truck, Max
knocked, and announced himself through the door. They
heard an electric wheelchair cross the room, and the click of
the lock.

Echo came in behind Max; Z, his back turned, was already
motoring back to the picture window. "So how'd it go, kid?"
he asked.

"I don't think this thing is too interested in your construction issues, Z. It's zoned strictly for Dimension X."

Z, his vision fixed on Oz, said "I saw the light show last
night. Was that your little girl?"

"Yeah. She says it took the form of a dragon because it was
looking for a dinosaur to play with. Does that make any sense
to you?"

Z shrugged. "It wants to play, huh? It plays a little rough."

"There's the pot calling the kettle black."

Z started to laugh, but it turned into cough.

"Z, it would be helpful if we knew what we're supposed to
be trying to get it to do. I mean, *really* trying to get it to do."

"I told you. I need it to cure me." Z half-turned his wheelchair in exasperation and finally caught sight of Echo. "Well,
hello there."

Echo nodded to Z, and then to Max. Max said, "Hello,
Juno."

The three—four?—of them stared at each other. Quite the
family reunion, Max thought. He watched the very features
of the face before him resolve into different shapes. He was
sure it had been Z's face when he'd first seen it, and perhaps

it still was, but only in the way a store front stays the same when a new owner, with a completely different agenda, takes over. Finally, the thing in the wheelchair spoke. "Can you see me?"

Echo nodded. Max had no idea what he was supposed to see.

A cruel smile of satisfaction crept across the face, followed seconds later by a look of utter desolation. A new voice spoke, not Juno's exactly, but hers in a lower, harsher register. "You went to a lot of trouble to get rid of Truck. You must have figured out that he doesn't know about me."

"Yeah, we figured if Truck learned you'd hijacked Z's body, he might get . . . ugly."

"When did *you* realize it?"

"It was Echo who realized it, when I told her about the herbs in the bathroom and the boots. I don't think *I* really bought it till about a minute ago."

Juno—Max thought the gesture was hers rather than Z's—indicated the sofa next to the wheelchair. "Sit down."

"Who exactly are we talking to?"

Juno smiled sourly. "Z is here, but feeling shy. At the moment, I have an arrangement much like yours with Echo."

"If we're going to discuss anything, the first thing you're gonna have to do is give Echo her voice back. Otherwise, we just walk the fuck out of here. And I won't forget to tell Truck who he's been taking orders from."

"I can't remove the curse myself," Juno answered hastily, "not in this condition. But I know how it can be done."

Max looked to Echo, who nodded to him, so he went on. "So, are you dead, or what?"

"If you mean, is my body dead, then yes. But there are other aspects of a person."

"Soul, spirit, shit like that?"

"Specifically, extra-dimensional . . . 'shit.' I once described magic to you, Echo, as a force like gravity that bends and reshapes reality. This force exists in other dimensions, dimensions you have the capacity to sense. You, Max, can't perceive them, even though a part of you exists in those other dimensions and even though the magic may manifest itself in the three dimensions you do perceive."

Max thought he'd just been deprived of a dimension, but he let her go on.

"There are a number of passageways into our world, but Oz is the one that is most attractive to this . . . entity. It is being drawn here as we might be drawn by some extra-dimensional force we call 'love' or 'God.'"

"You're saying it's here looking for its mate?" Max asked.

"No, that's too literal. I'm saying something we give off when we experience intense passion is attracting this thing, drawing it into our dimension. It isn't a creature and it isn't gravity, and it's not conscious in the way we are, but it's sentient. It does things with a purpose."

"What purpose?"

"As far as I can tell, its purpose is to suck up the output of human passion, as much of it as it can. But in doing so it distorts the boundaries, breaches the dimensions."

"So a man's hand might disappear or reappear?"

"Yes. Or a whole man might be drawn completely and permanently into a totally different dimensional space."

The black stains, Max thought. "Is that what death is?"

"No. But death is an interesting point. When you die, your bodies will decompose and your consciousnesses will scatter like rain water."

"Ouch."

"And this may happen sooner than you'd like, unless we help each other, Echo by drawing *it* to us, I by putting you on its back. If it comes all the way into this world, we can control it by manipulating how it receives those energies that attract it."

"So you say. How about if we just leave it alone? Does it go back where it came from?"

"Can you imagine what this place is going to look like when all the phantoms humanity has collected here come alive, from the MGM Lion to King Kong to the knights at the Excalibur, the mummies in this dump? Think of all mankind's mental creations as dry seeds. Well, we've watered the desert. The weddings, the divorces, the gambling, the lust, even just the excited click of heels on the pavement, that's all nourishment to this thing. It's been here, in some dimension adjacent to here, for tens of millions of years, and now it smells the coffee perking."

"And dangling Echo in front of it does what, exactly? If she's the bait, where's the hook?"

"That would be me." Juno pointed to herself, frowned, not liking what she saw. "Isn't it worth a try? If it could get Echo's speech back? Or your emotional commitment?" She looked hungrily out the window at Oz.

Max said, "And what happens if we can't control it?"

Juno shrugged. "You can't be worse off than dead, can you?"

"An interesting question. Here's another: why is it looking for dinosaurs?"

She didn't answer, and Echo, who had been sitting wide-eyed and absorbed, shot to her feet. Faced with her defection, Juno responded, "Perhaps the last time it was here, the last time it was drawn fully into our dimension, that's what the predominant life form was."

"And they became extinct shortly thereafter?"

This speculation Juno refused to answer at all.

20

"Bopper, we're not in Kansas anymore."
—Buddy Holly, five minutes after the plane crash.

When Echo and Max talked, he had to be completely focused on her to understand her. Few women got that kind of attention from a man. It was a rush, like holding a new-born baby for the first time and having it looking at you, knowing nothing else in the world.

If only Juno's curse on Max *could* be lifted, if he could actually love her . . . Oh, one wouldn't *necessarily* lead to the other, but he'd as much as said he wanted to try, hadn't he? And hadn't Juno promised that if Echo sang the creature into this world, she'd lift that curse?

Well, no, she hadn't. Juno might have only the vaguest notion of how to handle the creature. All Echo really knew was how desperate Juno was for this to happen.

The second Echo and Narcissus concert in Las Vegas may have been the poorest stage performance of their career together. Echo made a mental note never to perform on an evening when she also had to save the world.

"Some days," Crissy told her before Echo and Max slipped away from the post-concert party, "you suck. But it's still *you* sucking. It's still *your* show. And that's fucking great." And she was right, Echo thought. Even in its toughest moments, life was amazing. Did she have the courage to do whatever it took to prevent losing that for millions of other human beings?

She did, she thought, if it meant finally having Max.

* * *

They were in the back seat of a limo, a limo driven by a thug and commanded by a deranged dead woman wearing the body of a man who had tried to kill both of them, riding toward Oz, toward a creature from another dimension with enough power to destroy all life on Earth. *Where else but Vegas*, Echo thought. She could feel Max twitch and knew he was longing for a fix. She imagined him trying to describe this particular backslide at a Narcotics Anonymous meeting. He held her hand, both of them silent about the debate that had been raging between them all afternoon, a debate that had distracted them during the concert.

"Do what you have to do, kid," he finally whispered in her ear.

Like it was all her choice, like he had no responsibility in this. She slapped him, hard across the face, without knowing exactly why, except that maybe he was right, that maybe what she did was her own choice, would be on her forever. An uneducated (am I dumb?), semi-abandoned (what kind of values might a family have given me?), basically lawless (survival has its own rules, doesn't it?), hopelessly in love (hopelessly?) child (that's what I am, though I never really was) was supposed to decide whether to change the entire nature of reality (didn't really have a choice, because to not try would have repercussions too). She had to slap someone for this.

Max hugged her shoulder. Goddamn him.

When they reached the site, Truck unlocked the construction gate, and drove them right up the yellow brick road, past the wrecked clapboard house. The night was moonless, and the headlights that swept in curves along the golden road before them barely illuminated the encroaching forest of trees on either side. Truck pulled up to what would have been the lobby of the hotel, or the gates of the Emerald City.

"Isn't there supposed to be a witch's castle or something before we get to the Emerald City?" Max asked Truck.

"Last time we was here," he said, "there was." He pried himself out of the driver's seat and pulled the wheelchair from the trunk. Echo and Max got out cautiously.

Max cleared his throat. "So where is it?"

Truck looked around as he helped his boss into the wheelchair. "I think the forest covered it up."

Who would put a forest in front of a casino entrance, obscuring the vision that was supposed to draw in customers? Echo wondered. The forest was perhaps a correction made by something that took the old story literally, because it was in the minds and emotions of everyone who ever had come by this place.

Truck took a big, old-fashioned padlock key from his pocket, turned it in a keyhole that had looked purely ornamental, and pushed open the two enormous doors. Had they been designed to creak like that?

The lobby was the size of a football field and littered with the paraphernalia of a village marketplace. A blackened cave mouth, looking to Echo like one goddamn big roach motel, gaped where the registration desk might have been. Truck aimed his flashlight at it; the light seemed to get swallowed up without illuminating anything. To their left, a hallway began to glow a dull green.

Echo hummed a few bars from "Over the Rainbow," and then Max slapped out a military march version of "We're Off to See the Wizard" against his thighs, and the unlikely procession turned down the dimly lit hallway. "Kind of makes you want to click the heels of those cowboy boots, doesn't it?" Max asked.

Juno didn't answer, but, from behind her, Truck stared

down at the passenger in his wheelchair.

Almost immediately, Echo recognized the nature of the hallway. The walls lost their smoothness and took on the corrugated, intertwined complexion of the walls in the sub-basement of the Hard Rock Hotel where she'd first encountered the creature. Juno had Truck push her over to the wall, and when she began to examine the convoluted texture, it moved under her touch. She tried to sooth it with a whispering sound and the stroke of her fingers. This concerned Truck, who was thinking more along the lines of a good, swift kick. Or maybe it was the flickering of his flashlight that concerned him.

"If we pass a poppy field," Max said, "I'm stopping for a pick-me-up."

"Fine," Juno replied, using Z's voice. "You're not really essential to this operation. Unless you *want* to be able to love Echo."

The remark stung Echo, and she could see it shamed Max, and she wished she were able to give the old witch a piece of her mind. But Juno had taken care of that, hadn't she?

By now, the hallway, even the floor on which they walked, was composed entirely of the braided surfaces that marked the immediate presence of the beast, undulating in a peristaltic rut.

"So, exactly how does this work?" Max asked. "Echo sings, the creature gets real excited, comes completely into this dimension—and then you slam the door behind it? Is that it?"

"Something like that," Juno growled.

"And then we trap it? With what, exactly?"

Juno said, almost inaudibly, "With death."

Echo stopped humming.

"What?" Max asked.

"If it's attracted to human passion, animal passion, it

stands to reason it will be repelled by the opposite."

"Death. Is that the complete absence of passion?" Max mused. "I guess. What do you think, Truck?"

Truck was as silent as Echo.

"So you're carrying some form of death on you? Death concentrate, maybe? One death sure isn't gonna do it. It killed a bunch of people when it came through before and accidentally wiped out that construction crew. *Z?*"

They rounded a corner in the green gullet they'd been traveling down for some time now, *literally* down, on a slope so steep Truck had to exert considerable strength to keep the wheelchair from getting away. A set of doors, fractionally ajar, was visible twenty yards ahead.

"I'm going to offer it not just a life, but a soul that's been poisoned."

"Cursed, you mean? A soul that's been cursed by a dying witch, perhaps, with her own blood, and maybe the semen of her murderer? That *would* be pretty anti-life, wouldn't it?"

"Shut up, you little prick." They were at the doors. Max and Echo looked at each other. They pushed the doors open.

Echo had been half-hoping Truck would have to fight off the Tin Man, or a few flying monkeys, but then it occurred to her that perhaps he *was* the Tin Man. No, that would be Max. The Scarecrow?

In front of them now stood a stupendous replication of the great throne of Oz. And off to the side of the huge chamber fluttered a ceiling-to-floor green drapery.

"Showtime," Max whispered. Echo wished he'd take charge the way he usually did just before they went on stage, wished he'd give her some sort of cue to assure her that her instincts were right. But they had to be. She could have him forever, if she could seduce this thing all the way into their world.

She started to sing, the same keening song it had responded to before.

The curtains rippled more noticeably. A wailing sound
blared from an enormous gramophone speaker next to the
empty throne. Or *was* it empty? As Echo picked up the re-
sponsive tones and scatted along with them and ahead of
them, a shape, as yet indistinct, seemed to intimate itself
there.

She was vaguely aware of Truck, behind her, pushing Juno's wheelchair up toward the curtain, and of Max, standing
at her side, transfixed by her song, gaping at the throne,
where the shape remained insubstantial—though Echo now
had no doubt it was there. The power was all hers. This was
the song she had been born to sing, as Juno herself must have
known for some time.

Echo raised her voice, soloed mightily, sounds full of hope
and love, the most beautiful sounds she could remember having sung. And the thought that such beauty was needed to
attract this . . . creature, upset her greatly.

The curtain began to part. Truck took his hands off the
wheelchair and stood erect, his nostrils flared like the barrels
of a shotgun. With her frail hands, Juno was struggling to remove the cowboy boots.

Echo's voice soared. She realized suddenly that Max was
holding her hand, and wondered if the spell that separated
them might already be weakening. She sang out with all her
heart, bringing the thing, the parts already in this world and
the parts that were not, bringing them all into this throne
room.

The shape on the throne began to resolve itself. It was a
dozen feet tall, at least, and glowing red and black against the
green of the throne. Its eyes coalesced, dozens of them, fierce
and sentient, each more like the eye of a storm than of a

beast, eyes that were mouths, too, so that if you were seen, you were eaten.

"Pay no attention to the monster behind the curtain," Max whispered.

But even as Echo struggled to consolidate her own connection with the creature, she became aware of another presence. She felt it as a backbeat, growing louder, hotter, usurping her song. And she saw Juno craning forward from the wheelchair, saw an insane, jubilant greed in her eyes, a burning hatred. Was it all a lie? A con, to get Echo to bring the creature to her, *for* her, Echo the crimson cape, Juno the hidden sword?

She knew that what they were seeing was not the thing itself, remembered inanely the story of the blind men, each attempting to identify an elephant by touching a single part of its anatomy. That reminded her of Terry, Terry who would have known what she needed to do. So then she knew what she needed to do.

She poured her intensity into the song, her passion, and as the thing seemed to reach out for her with impossibly long arms, her tone quickly changed, began a discordant shriek.

It shrank back, confused.

Now Echo was pouring out a determined hopelessness, informed by her own sense of irreversible loss. The curtain had parted completely, and Echo could not help seeing, behind the throne, the black maw of a place humans were not meant to be. It pulsed without movement, boiled without heat.

Juno stood from the wheelchair, held both boots above her head, and shrieked, "Z, plug up the asshole of the world!"

"You bitch!" With a scream, Truck launched himself and the wheelchair at Juno, striking her from behind so that she fell back into the chair, even as they were both pulled forward toward the blackness.

Echo wasn't sure if, at the last moment, Truck tried to arrest his own motion and was simply drawn forward by the force of the creature slamming itself back into its own dimension. It didn't look that way to her.

The ground trembled beneath them, pitching Max and Echo to the floor. When Echo looked up, the room was black, save for Truck Stop's flashlight, rocking slightly on the floor, reflecting off an unfinished concrete wall.

Echo wished as never before that she could somehow get inside Max's head, speak directly to him. *You have got to know, in the middle of all this bullshit, that I love you. That I always have and always will. Don't forget, ever, that you had this connection with another human being. At your worst moment, remember this.*

She tried to speak, but could not. Max held her in cold arms.

Part IV
The Overworld

21

They tell me not to lose control
As they take it from me.
So I organize my thoughts like bullets
Passing through my body/gun.
I imagine an expansive mausoleum
Of platinum angles, a revolution, and
Your song in my mouths.

—Max

It was just like TV, in a way: with commercial interruptions, you had forty-seven minutes to save the world, and then you got your ass back on the reality bus. In their case, it was a bus waiting to drive them down to Phoenix. They rolled on out of the bright lights, into the darkness of the desert, and later, while Max pretended to sleep, Daniel told Echo she'd missed this really cool light show from somewhere at the end of the strip.

In Phoenix the next afternoon, Lucy found Max roughing out a new tune for Echo. "Stop the Robert Smith shit," she said. "The Cure have never had a song hit number one." She was going back to LA that evening, and thus was meddling overtime.

"But they've had a twenty-year run," Max pointed out. "You'll make your money eventually, Luce."

"Yeah? You think you'll be here in twenty years, Max?"

He didn't answer. He'd been planning to call the song "Different Lives," but who was he kidding?

They opened for Inner War at Desert Sky Pavilion, an enormous outdoor amphitheater where, even at night, it was a hundred degrees in the audience and a hundred and five on stage.

When Johnny Lang's opening act failed to show the following night, Max and Echo also got to play the Celebrity theater, a circular venue with a rotating stage that made Echo mildly seasick; she sang most of their songs in the aisles. Then they were off to Tucson the following evening to rejoin Inner War at a great old indoor theater called the Rialto. After that, Albuquerque, Denver, Minneapolis, Ann Arbor . . .

The first CD was doing well, made it into the top ten on both the rock and jazz charts. They seldom did TV shows, since Echo couldn't talk and Max wouldn't show up sober, but they did play on a *few* late-night programs, including *Saturday Night Live*. Groupies began to hit on both of them, with erratic success. Private investigators from the scandal sheets scoped their conversations with hidden microphones, hoping Echo's speechlessness would be revealed as a publicity stunt; they at best came away with weird stories based on Max's drunken comments, comments about dinosaurs and the increasingly bizarre electrical storms being reported around the world.

Larry King invited them to a panel program about muteness, where Echo might have availed herself of the free services of the world's greatest experts on hysterical paralysis and speech therapy, but they declined. Larry sent Max a matching set of suspenders and necktie anyway, and Max wore them on stage, sans shirt, the next night. Lucy made sure King received a video clip.

"How do you know when you're famous?" Daniel asked them while the three waited for their food at a truck stop café.

"When the waitress wants you to sign something other than a check," Max replied.

"Remember that time the waitress at the Café du Monde had you sign her breast? You told her you were only fifteen, so it wasn't legal tender."

Dear Max,

You used to tell me how you felt most alone in a crowd because somehow you weren't like other people. Being in here makes me feel like I'm not any kind of person at all, just food for some huge, grazing beast. I feel like I'm being chewed up, day after day, but never spit out. Someone called prison the Belly of the Beast. It smells that way. It feels worse. I'm beaten and raped and the sickest part is I can see they're not even interested, they're bored doing it to me, but they do it anyway because I'm a cop. Was a cop.

The second Echo and Narcissus CD debuted at number two, and was the best-selling CD in the world for two months. They headlined their own concert tour this time. But the personal relationship of Max and Echo was strained to the breaking point. They rarely spent time together when they weren't rehearsing or performing. While Echo retired into a persistent, respectable privacy, Max was frequently featured on the cover of supermarket tabloids escorting movie stars, models, musicians, and millionaires, *usually* female. He was rumored to have impregnated this or that happily married starlet; in actuality, many of the celebrity rumors were engineered by Lucy. Those close to Max knew he was more likely to turn down the advances of the rich and famous to spend a weekend of lust in a motel room with some waitress or groupie.

Max's orgies were legend. Reports were that you could have anything you wanted there. Including him, if you didn't mind waiting in line, didn't mind looking into his eyes, eyes desperate and distant, as if belonging to someone in a sensory deprivation chamber, straining to hear the most distant sound.

Some good news: to show the citizens of Calfornia he is Tough On Crime, the governor has ordered inmates to work on chain gangs rather than fritter away the taxpayers' money sitting in cells waiting to die. A dozen of us were shackled together and transported under heavy guard into the desert. There was a moment when one of the guards said "We're gonna clean up this piece of shit desert," and I was thinking, Cruel joke, we're going to dig our own graves.

Then our hands were unshackled, but not the legs, and there was no way we could be given gardening tools, all potential weapons. So the Dirty Dozen hand-weeded the desert for eight hours without a break, under the scrutiny of eight guards itching to deploy some nonlethal buckshot, while the bus driver slept in the shade of his bus, and motorists on car phones called in the sighting ("Dead Men Gardening") to a local radio station that delights in tracking such events.

A light rain began to fall.

It was the first rain I'd felt in two and a half years. When I realized I was standing with my face raised, my eyes and mouth wide open, I looked around in embarrassment, but the other cons, hardened inmates all, were doing exactly the same thing.

It was an amazing day. The sound of traffic on the freeway, the flinty scent of the desert air after the rain, the sky, the wind—the horizon, for God's sake! No bars. You can't imagine what it meant to me. When the wind died down, I thought I could hear children playing.

After this first day of the new Get Tough plan, inmates deluged the guards with queries about the next work detail. We were told the governor was rethinking the experiment.

*   *   *

The interviews Max did were never straight, although the reporter he was seducing rarely realized it. One woman wrote in the introduction to a lengthy *Playboy* interview, about Max's "personal philosophy of compassionate cynicism," supposing that a stack of unopened letters from a prison in California on his end table was an indication of just how overwhelming fame was for this sensitive boy. She asked him if he believed in God ("Not in any god that seems to believe in me."), and what it had been like to come of age in Echo Park, with its now famous *Bakanas* and $E^2=MC$ graffiti ("People there are really into relativity.").

When a reviewer from *Modern Woman* flat out accused Max of being the poster boy of sexual predation and a destroyer of social values, Max gave her his innocent, confused smile, and explained that he agreed, and that his own sex life was greatly exaggerated.

"In fact, all of this fame is a big turn off for me," he told her. "I rarely even get aroused any more. Oh, I don't mean to be vulgar. It's just, for some reason, I feel like maybe you'll actually listen to me, where all the others were just looking for quotes and scandal. I was thinking about this just before you arrived, in fact. Last night—this is really embarrassing—last night I had the first erotic dream I've had in years. It's a very ordinary dream, really. Maybe that's the only amazing thing about it. Don't print this, okay? You promise? I just need to talk about it." (*Maybe* he pressed her hand reassuringly here, just briefly, as she later wrote; she no doubt remembered, although he didn't.) "When I step back from this dream, it's really pretty unoriginal, yet I can't unscramble what it means to me. In this dream, I'm in some sort of a crowded area, maybe a post-concert show or a press conference, where people are crammed together and it's dark.

There's a woman in front of me, not real young, not old, short curly blond hair, on the thin side, wearing a tasteful skirt and blouse—like the way you're dressed. She seems to be casually bumping against me, and the crowd is pushing us around a bit, but after a while I realize she's leaning back against me. And then, duh, while I'm still thinking about how to react, she slips a hand back there. Eventually we make love, right there, standing up. If anyone else at the press conference notices, they don't say anything. The sex is urgent, but drawn out and slow.

"When I woke up, I thought, well, that's pretty reminiscent of the old zipless fuck scenario from *Fear of Flying*. But making love to this woman didn't feel that way psychologically. It wasn't the same anonymity, the pleasure divorced from all consequences. The whole point seemed to be that we had this mutual need, that we were together in some emotional sense even if in no other. But I can't quite get a handle on what the difference is. Maybe I'm just denying my own crudeness, and there is no difference. I was just struck by how vivid this was, given the usual half-dozen-positions-with-the-cheerleaders nature of my every-night pornography, back when I used to dream about sex all the time. I really wanted to discuss this dream with Echo, because it was so arousing, but I know she would immediately be pissed off because it wasn't her in the dream. It would reinforce her fear that I don't want her, just every stranger I meet.

"So, any ideas? I mean, I think the thing I'm trying to get at is, it didn't feel at all impersonal. It was *very* personal on some limbic level, that's what was cool about it, important about it. The easy analysis is the gratification without commitment thing, sexual/emotional free lunch. But that's what I have the cheerleaders for. Is my dream just an aesthetic throwback to the sixties? And what is the public component?

I really don't think it's voyeurism/braggadocio; I hate having sex in public. Have you ever had sex at a press conference? Really?

"Oh, sure, I know you were just kidding. I'd like to believe the dream is about connectedness to people, to society, rather than a denial of it, which is what porno is, an imaginary denial of rules and cosmic social dues. Maybe it's a way of imagining that this person, this experience, is simply out there. Or that the quality of sensual need is the secret glue (yuck, sorry) that holds society together. I don't know. I don't usually think about these things. Any help would be appreciated. How did it feel when you had sex at the press conference?"

Your dream, he didn't say to her, is about being a star. That's why you imagine fucking someone at a press conference. All reporters are star fuckers, in one way or another. You'll fuck me now, and tell your friends about it, because we both have such a twisted sense of what's important, what's valuable. Only I'm a couple steps ahead of you, because I've known for years what I'm worth. Exactly nothing.

The only way I can survive the rapes and the beatings is to imagine they mean something, that they're happening for some reason. When I'm being raped I think of you, of our first time, when I didn't realize how much it must have hurt you, because what I intended, what I wanted to give you wasn't pain, it was love. So then I think, This pain can't be all bad.

I had that dream again the other night, where my wife and son and I are coming out of the movies and we run into you, and she knows right away who you are. You didn't say anything, it was me, I just couldn't look away, couldn't lie about how I felt about you. My wife and I argue, and my son's so upset that he runs out in the street and gets hit by a car . . . God, that was just a dream, wasn't it?

* * *

On the same day the tabloids reported Echo's secret funding of a home for unwed mothers in Athens, Georgia, their headline was Max's arrest for prostitution. Accepting drugs for sex could be charged that way, according to a St. Louis prosecutor. The charges were dropped when Lucy launched a counter-campaign investigating the prosecutor's questionable past and current political aspirations.

Around this time, Max bought Echo a Mexican parrot named Tequila with whom she had perfectly circular conversations, and Echo sent him back two smaller but similarly colored lovebirds called Treachery and Deceit who bit anyone who got near them. This was before anyone but Max and Echo knew of their split.

Split? Maybe, but Echo refused to give it up and Max refused to let it hold him. He agreed to a serious confrontation at a restaurant, where Echo could at least be sure he would be no more than badly drunk. "I am so excited," he slurred as soon as he saw her, "my socks are on fire."

She could see he was trying to destroy himself, because he could not face this moment honestly. She had written a letter telling him what she felt in a way he couldn't pretend to misunderstand, and knew she could force him to read it when it was delivered face to face. "I want you," it said. "I want us, who have grown up alone, to be a family."

Max sighed, unable to rally his sarcasm. "We've had Z and Juno as our parental models," he said. "Them, or maybe the parents *they* betrayed—that sort of shit goes on, from generation to generation. How can that make you feel like having a family? What fucking chance would we possibly have?"

When she heard later that evening he'd been hospitalized for acute intoxication, Echo forced herself not to go to the hospital. At least from the nurses he can get sex, she thought.

* * *

Reincarnation: I know you sort of believe in that. I've seen so much shit lately, I feel like I've been reincarnated as bacteria in a baboon's lower intestine. Remember Buddha Burgers? Wish I knew why my karma sucked so bad.

God I need a break from this. It's not a matter of being afraid of anything in particular, more like everybody, everything, every minute itself. I'm nearly broken. I know they probably won't let you visit me, probably don't even give you my letters, or you would have been here. But a letter from you would help a lot.

Love,

Michael

Max's modeling career went to hell before his music career did, but for different reasons (not including the fact that Lucy controlled both). When his drug addictions left Max haggard and hollow-eyed, Lucy was able to shift him to new clients who worked with that look to sell fashionable crap to rich teenagers who fancied themselves dissipated. But the problem developed when he simply didn't show up at all for his shoots.

In music, Max could get away with being unreliable; it was like being fashionably late for dinner, as long as you were an honored guest. But when he refused to write for Echo and she refused to perform with him, Lucy had to pick one over the other, and Echo's reliability and greater artistic flexibility determined the choice. Hell, Echo would have sung Christmas carols at the White House, or danced during halftime at the Super Bowl. In Max's view, those kinds of gigs were shit. Nobody cared about the music. People weren't there to have their emotional guts twisted or their sexual chains yanked. Fuck it. He'd rather play in a biker bar. Which he often did, usually for free, Fed-Exing Lucy a six pack as her ten percent of what he'd drunk.

So there was no third CD with Echo, and Max's only solo, *The Myth of Sisyphus*, while a huge underground hit, became so tangled up in a contract dispute with Lucy's agency, it never sold in mainstream stores.

And Max didn't see Echo again until the Virgin Mary appeared over Echo Park.

22

How many lived lies ago
did I sink too low
to not lay down?
                    —Max

Echo was never so nothing as when she had nearly everything. Her *Elvis's Dead Twin* CD, on which she sang the female photo negative of the white man singing the black man's
music, went platinum on the Internet the afternoon it was released. The record company people who had been screaming
that she had to tour to promote the album, because everybody toured to promote an album, discovered that her complete invisibility was an even greater promotional tool. Questions of her whereabouts, of what she was doing, of why she
had disappeared from public view, became matters of public
debate. Rumors of Echo-sightings became media events. A
half-dozen web sites purported to track her movements, and,
because their information differed wildly, spawned e-fights,
hacking, and lawsuits. Speculation was rampant: she had died
in a motorcycle wreck shortly after completing the CD; she
had been dead for months, communing with Elvis, and singing through a medium; she had throat cancer and her voice
was being reconstructed by a computer which actually "sang"
all her new work; she was crippled or deformed by plastic
surgery that had tried to turn her into Elvis (or McCartney or
B.B. King); she was really twin sisters, or a brother and sister
(which explained her incredible vocal range); a certain crime
syndicate out of New Orleans had put a price on her head;
and/or space travelers had taken her back to her own planet,
where everyone could sing like that.

In truth, Echo did not appear because she felt a voice was all she was. *I remember when I had a self*, she thought. *Back when I was in New Orleans. Maybe I was a runaway, with no money, and no plan, but I had a self.*

She remembered almost killing the umbra with a song, before she realized how they fed off her emotions. It must have been right after the first time she played with Narc, and she'd been trying to write her own song that she could sing to Max, to show him that she had her own style, that, even if she *could* be any singer she wanted to be, she still preferred to be herself with him. But the words vanished in the air. Juno, preparing a bouquet of herbs at the other end of the room, didn't even hear her. And when Echo looked down at the umbra, crowded around her as she sat cross-legged on the floor, she saw they were growing increasingly pale. Something told her she was poisoning them. She stopped, and they slowly slid away, and she didn't try singing her own song again for a long time.

"Mice don't domesticate cats," Juno had once said, always trying to warn her away from Max without telling her why. The warning had only made Max more irresistible; there's nothing like the truth to sucker you in.

Gibson's was a trashy club on the edge of a surprisingly nice, grassy mall in Tempe, a university 'burb of Phoenix. Max was playing a gig with Dr. DeCyst, a local punk band founded by a plastic surgeon. Max's gigs these days were unadvertised at his insistence. He claimed it was a precaution against Michael tracking him down; more likely it was his own gamesmanship, the kick he got when people who weren't expecting anything special realized it was Max on stage.

Echo had gotten the booking information through Lucy's network. She kept her visit top secret, of course, fearful she'd be recognized, even in the dark glasses and wig. But no one noticed, not in line at the concert and not in the crowd inside, and why *should* they have? No one ever expected to see her live these days. One guy, high on something, claimed to recognize her, but he insisted she was Halle Berry.

Inside, Gibson's was remarkably dingy, close to a thousand people packed into a venue that sat a few hundred. There was a bar on the ground floor and another in the balcony, and as Echo stood at the railing looking down, she thought she probably could jump onto the stage without hurting herself. Well, without killing herself.

As the balcony became more and more crowded, as Echo gained personal knowledge of the sexual equipage of a variety of young men struggling past her with drinks for their dates, she wondered if she were doing the right thing, wished she were smarter. Where was Terry when you needed him? If she walked out of here now and went back to Echo Park, would she find him sitting on the stoop, invisible to nearly everyone but her?

The club went black. A moment later, when the stage lights came up, a team of hospital-gowned musicians strode to the front of the stage and tore into their first number.

And there was Max, black leather pants and black muscle shirt, black wraparound shades and black motorcycle boots, clove dangling from his lips, playing rhythm guitar off to the side, doing nothing to attract attention except being Max.

The lead singer, a little blond—well, blond yesterday, pink-haired today—was about Echo's shape and size. She wore a pornographically tiny nurse's uniform and threw the cap into the audience half way through the first song. Most eyes were on her, but Echo's were on Max, pure ache coming with every chord he played. His white-blond hair was streaked with black, which made him look all the blonder. He stared casually, curiously out at the audience, but would have had to tilt his head almost straight back to see Echo fifteen feet above him. He paid no attention to the pink and white singer, except to crack a smile at the end of the song when she gyrated wildly in front of him and then flung herself on the floor at his feet.

Dr. DeCyst's part was finished, but Max took up where they left off, the guitar leaping in his hands, screaming down at the woman below him in wild sexual crescendos. She writhed in ecstasy; Max played on, solo; and Echo heard the people around her begin to buzz with excitement. "That looks like Max. That's Max! I told you that looked like Max!"

Two minutes later, Max slammed his guitar into silence with the palm of his hand, and the crowd erupted. The singer, who had wound herself around his leg and was gazing directly up into his crotch, buried her face in him, and the group's male lead announced with great pleasure, their new friend and guest for the evening, yadda yadda yadda. Of course, in order for there to be an evening, someone would have to pry nursie off Max so she could return to the microphone.

She'll do, Echo thought, pushing her way through the crush of fans to the door. *How did the line in that movie go? I'll make her a proposition she can't confuse . . .*

Waiting naked in the darkened hotel room, sipping from the bottle of Jack Daniels on the nightstand, Echo felt the perspiration drip between her small, fierce breasts. She was tight, worse even than pre-show jitters. At least on stage, she instinctively knew what audiences wanted; now she was dealing with the one audience she had never been able to please.

She heard a bump against the door, and the security card sliding into the lock, and knew Pinkie was keeping her end of the bargain. She could fuck Max another time—a solo contract with Echo's label was a career maker.

Echo had drawn her chair over by the veiled window, the darkest corner of the room. She was looking away from the door when it opened and the two figures spilled in from the hallway, the small woman incongruously supporting the taller male. Both were giggling, and Echo thought briefly that this might be easier as a threesome. But she wanted him to herself this once.

Max fell—or was deposited—face-down on the bed, and Echo quickly moved out of the corner. The little singer jumped when she felt Echo's hand on her arm, but she didn't resist as Echo gently pushed her out the door.

In the blackness of the room, Echo knelt at the foot of the bed and pulled off Max's boots and socks.

"Don't worry," he said, "I'm not too drunk." In a peculiar tone, he added, "I'm never too drunk, only not drunk enough."

"Never too drunk," Echo whispered.

"You've heard that too?" he laughed. Then he said, "Condom. It's my only rule. There's one in my pocket." He rolled over, and Echo moved her hand to his crotch just long enough to pull down his zipper. He arched his back to help her get his pants and briefs off.

Echo found the condom in his front left pocket, and slid her bare body up his legs, cupping his half-erect member in her hands, then her lips.

"Banana fana fo fana . . . " he sang, as she removed the condom from its foil wrapper, and applied it to him with her mouth.

He didn't notice when she bit a hole through the end.

And then she was on top of him, and he was too drunk to know if he was wearing a condom or a football helmet.

Later, as Max slept, Echo went into the bathroom, closed the door behind her, and turned on the light. She leaned across the sink, looked at herself in the mirror. On the sink was a small paper box that held contact lens solution. Artificial Tears, it was called. Who the hell needs those? she wondered.

23

*At the point where mental masturbation becomes self-rape
the seed of poetry is sown.*

—Max

It was odd finding himself in Phoenix as often as he did.
Max didn't like the place so much as feel drawn to it, enough
to take several gigs a year there. In Phoenix, for some reason,
he had the sense of being in a place where he wasn't so sure
he was worthless, although he couldn't have said why.

Otherwise he gravitated to LA, SF and NY, because that's
where the clubs were. No city with a name more than two
letters long had enough clubs, except maybe Chicago, which
was too cold. He never planned to show his face in New
Orleans again.

He stayed away from Echo Park as well. The news from
there was very weird: astral visitations, mass hallucinations,
mutilation deaths. Maybe Terry could have kept the lid on,
maybe not. Mostly Max stayed away because he didn't want
to run into Michael.

What was he going to do, apologize? Apologize for killing
the man's partner? For the loss of his wife, his kids, his career? Apologize for not being able to love *him*, either?

Michael's jail time had had something to do with stolen
property, a pricey necklace checked out from the evidence
room and never put back. Got nailed pretty hard.

Max never did find out when and if Michael was getting
out, and figured it didn't much matter. Cops don't do well in
prison.

Tonight Max had played the Rhythm Room, a Phoenix
dive that had to have once been somebody's cinder block club

house, a tight little club, like an ugly woman who doesn't give a shit and is gonna dance her ass off anyway. Max had agreed to the gig because a lot of other acts he really liked had played there, Shamika Copeland just a couple weeks ago. Now, here he was, standing in the pitch black of the parking lot, smoking a clove, staring at the stars and wondering what the hell had happened to his, when this big fucking Lincoln pulls in, comes right toward him. Max didn't move very fast, too relieved to move fast, relieved the vehicle wasn't a cop car.

Only one guy got out, but he was very big. Hispanic, darkly handsome, cold. Perhaps forty. He had on a great-looking suit, which meant he wasn't afraid of anybody in this trashy neighborhood. Not a good sign for Max, whom he walked right up to.

"My employer wants to speak with you."

Could it be Michael? Why had he been thinking of Michael tonight? "If I say, *Speak for yourself, John Alden*, are you going to have a clue as to what I'm talking about?"

"This woman is very beautiful. A nice person."

So not Michael. "So the answer would be no. No."

"She said I should bring you back to her house even if I had to offer you a million dollars."

"Offer, or pay?"

"You will come with me."

"Fuck you, handsome."

As the fist he never saw smashed into his stomach, Max had a peculiarly, perversely happy thought: at last a man who isn't taken in by my fucking charm.

He felt a little less amused when he was in his second minute of not being able to breathe.

The car was going about forty by the time Max started feeling oxygenated enough to move. He continued to lie on the back seat, however. It was a nice, soft leather. "The back seat," he said. "Is that an insult? I'm not dangerous enough to be thrown in the trunk? You don't want me in the front where you can keep an eye on me?"

"Yes. No. No."

"Yes, no, no. Is this an oral test?"

"Sorry. My employer is very precise about words. My opinion is that you're just a harmless asshole."

"Thanks . . . I think. What's your name? Code name, number, whatever."

"Roberto."

"Roberto?"

"What's wrong with that?" the big man asked placidly.

"On you, it's good," Max said. "Roberto, did you ever work in the, uh, music industry?"

He shrugged.

"For someone named Lucy?" Someone who was precise about words—as in broken contracts. "Hey, how'd you get those bodies out of The Whisky?"

"Wires come out of amplifiers and speakers real easy. What's left is mostly empty space."

"You fit Nemo into a speaker?"

"The big guy? He was a two-speaker job. *You* I could fit into an amp."

Live by the sword, die by the sword, Max thought. "You taking me to Lucy?"

"She said not to tell you. You might not want to come."

"She was right, I *didn't* want to come. But you can tell me now, see? Now that I've been kidnaped, it's exciting. I can't find out what this is about without going all the way."

"You're *being* kidnaped," corrected Roberto, insisting again on verbal precision. "And you might be afraid I'm going to kill you."

"You had to mention that."

Max sat up, leaned back, looked out the window, all the while keeping both hands on his stomach. Mostly, the only driveways on this main thoroughfare were for gated communities hidden behind eucalypti and giant oleanders. The road they turned off on went up Camelback Mountain, up over sandy, dung-shaped humps, elegantly littered with two-hundred-year-old saguaros, blooming ocotillo that looked like fireworks escaping from the underworld, and kazillion-dollar houses on lots the size of golf courses.

"I am so glad this isn't one of those bush kidnapings," Max said, "where they take you from a nice place to a shitty place. Kidnapers would get a lot more cooperation if they all did it your way."

Roberto didn't respond, and Max reflected that he hadn't precisely asked a question.

"Uh, Roberto, that's not actually a castle, is it?"

"How do you define castle?"

"Turrets with slits to shoot arrows through. High stone walls. Moat."

"That's not a moat. It's a wash."

"Can we agree that it's a *natural* moat? I'm not arguing that the drawbridge is superfluous."

Roberto played with a handful of security dinguses on a panel where his armrest should have been, and the drawbridge came down six inches in front of the Lincoln. As a curved gravel drive brought them to a black oak door set in a huge stone arch, they rolled to a stop. Max was still fiddling with the handle when Roberto let him out of the car.

"I've changed my mind; take me back," Max said.

Roberto didn't respond, but led him through the oak door (the man knew a *lot* of security codes) and down a beautifully tiled hallway into a high-ceilinged room with a solid glass wall that looked down on the city lights of Phoenix, a town that looked a lot better at night from a rich person's living room.

From Echo's living room.

She was sitting comfortably in the depths of an armchair. Probably glad to be held, Max thought. And the room they were in only *seemed* like a normal living room because she was at ease in it. She was flanked by a bank of new electronic decks, listening to Billie Holiday's "Strange Fruit" laid over her own vocal riffs about how "The fruits of murder/went a lot further/since they did it to her," and in the background, the sound of wind blowing through poplar trees, and even further back Max swore he could hear himself, distantly singing something that sounded like "Yes, We Have No Bananas," and "Banana bana bo bananananana . . ." while Echo rapped on "Nemesis/he got pissed/at Narcissus/'cause he loved no one./God with a hard on/gives no pardon/ya gotta love someone." Where the hell had *that* come from?

Music had caught up to him, he realized. Even his own was happening without him now, so he could just fade away, no responsibility.

"Do I get my million dollars now?" he asked.

"I said offer, not pay, remember?" Roberto smiled.

Max sat on a couch a dozen feet from Echo. It felt odd; he'd almost always sat with his knees six inches from her, or closer, and now he needed this coffee table between them like the principal's desk. She looked good, he thought, the white hair still cropped close, her face just a touch fuller now that she was in her twenties. Her figure might be fuller, too, couldn't tell, she was wearing one of those shapeless caftan things. He wondered if she always looked sad these days, or just when *he* dropped by.

"I'm glad you got hold of me," he said, "even if it *was* literally, because there's something, just one thing, that I wanted to tell you. Mostly these days I'm too wasted to pick up the phone and talk to Lucy to get your number. No, let me be precise, *always* too wasted. I should have hired one of these," he said, pointing to Roberto, "to beat me up and drag me to your house."

Echo looked at him.

"Ah, the one thing. I wanted to tell you how proud I was of you for doing something worthwhile. Not this shit," he waved his arm at the sumptuous room. "I mean, that night in Vegas when you saved the world."

She shook her head sadly.

"No," Max insisted. "See, that's exactly why I knew I had to tell you. You think, well, I was given this gift and I was lucky enough to be able to use it for something really important, so what's the big deal? The big deal is that you did do it. You saved a lot of people. Some of them probably were even *worth* saving. You are a fucking rock, Echo. You are the best . . . "

He trailed off, looked around for a drink or a line. "I, on the other hand, am shit. Don't think I haven't wanted to do *something*, but I can't figure out what. People say, hey, why don't you do a free concert to raise money for junkies? They say that because they *are* junkies, the people I know. But it's not lost on me that I could be making a ton of money and giving it away to poor people, or whatever."

Echo's eyes moved to a framed t-shirt on the wall. It was from a charity gig he'd done for AIDS victims.

"Yeah, well, that was self-serving unloading of guilt. I've probably given half the country AIDS by being a role model for the promiscuous. Basically, I think all I'd be doing is conning a bunch of jerks into letting me use some of their money to put a band aid on a festering sore. I'd spoil it just by being in the picture, giving them an excuse *not* to do the right thing. You follow me? Of course not, *I* don't even follow me. Nice frame, by the way. Goes with Roberto's suit. Oh, I'm sorry for being such an asshole. I *have* missed you. You're the only one I've ever met who knows how full of shit I am." He started to cry.

Roberto brought him a glass of Scotch, but Max pushed it away, sighed, and apologized.

"She wants to know if you've heard about what's going on in Echo Park," Roberto said.

"You mean the, duh, Madonna that people have been seeing in the sky there? The big floating face in the clouds that's been on the cover of every newspaper in the country for the past month? Except we know it's not the Mother of Christ, don't we? We know that face. It's frigging Juno."

"She wants to know—"

"Don't fucking interpret for me! I was interpreting for her when . . . when she could still talk!" Max slumped back on the couch. "So she wants to know if I'll go there with her, right?"

"Well, if you already know, why are you asking me?"

"It's weird," Max said, "I usually know these things right off, but you have *got* to be gay."

Roberto was unruffled. Echo sighed to get Max's attention, which Max realized she should not have had to do, except that he was avoiding her in order to . . . avoid everything else. "Hey, Echo, I'm sorry. I've read the news, too. Not just about Juno, but about all the deaths. The human sacrifice stories at the *Bakanas*. You don't think Terry's involved with that shit, do you?"

Echo shook her head. "Don't think Terry's . . . "

"Even alive," Max finished for her. "But Juno's there, somehow, riding another creature, maybe? Something that gives her power? And you think we can stop her?"

Echo shrugged.

"Now I really wish I hadn't said all that save-the-world shit, 'cause that's what we're talking about again here, isn't it? Except if you and I go in there, we're just going to get killed. Juno will know what you're planning. You'd be better off taking Roberto. I mean, I'll go, but . . . What *are* you planning?"

Echo handed him a sheet of paper that looked like it had just come off a desktop print shop. It was a flyer advertising a "Concert to Save Echo Park," featuring the long-awaited reunion of Echo and Narcissus.

24

Shoot crack like sunlight through me
and I won't crack.
Tie me to the molester's bed
and I will wedge myself in myself.
                                    —Max

Max looked at the vacant stoop, the bricked-up doorway of the old subterranean apartment. "Well, Sisyphus, the Jew has wandered back, and where the hell are you? *You're* the one who almost had a sense of purpose."

He was in Echo Park a week before he had to be, because if he had to come back, he might as well get used to it, get back to what was real to him. Terry would have gotten a big blind laugh out of that.

But what to do? If Terry still existed, where would he be? Rolling a rock up Beverly Hills?

Construction already was going on in the park. What Echo had envisioned was far more than an acoustic guitar set for the grass-and-blanket crowd sharing picnic baskets on a cool evening. The concert was, after all, her first appearance in years and had acquired the status of a Beatles reunion, including the dead ones. That meant considerable security concerns. Roberto undoubtedly was securing the beachhead, over in the Park—

It was then he saw it, newly painted on an unrented billboard across the street. Uncoiled, the snake would have been fifty feet long. Its blind eyes dominated the center of the whitewashed board. And down in the corner, what did that say? He started across to get a closer look. There was a low-rider drifting down the street, and it stopped for him, only to suddenly jack itself up on some psycho suspension, so that its grill looked like a mouth, and Max had to smile at the Hispanic kids who'd made him jump.

When he got up to the billboard, Max saw, painted in the left-hand corner, a notice for an AA meeting. A weird-looking notice with skulls and shit, but it did say AA, and gave a place nearby and a time that evening, and Max thought, well, it's one thing to play wasted at the nothing gigs he'd been doing the past year, no one expected him to be tight with the other musicians if he was guest of honor, but this thing with Echo was going to be a major production, giant stage set, special effects, back-up people he'd never played with before (not counting the ubiquitous Daniel). It might be a good idea to, well, cut back a little, get away from this apartment building where all he'd ever done was score, and why not get his ass to a meeting—especially if it was being run by Terry the Snake?

The AA meeting was being held in the basement of a bar, which Max had to admit was as novel an approach as the skull and cross-bones posters, but then AA types were never shy about innovation and improvisation—as long as you took your twelve steps one day at a time. Only, when Max arrived, there *was* no AA meeting, at least not what he'd expected. The banner, stretched across the podium, said "Alternative Apocalypse."

Well, that's a cheap trick to get an audience, he thought. Then he thought, My main objective is still to find Terry, but this might be an entertaining meeting after all.

The place filled up, chairs all occupied by the weirdest people, mostly black, but some dangerous-looking Hispanics and even a couple whites. Standing room was scarce.

Eventually, and without warning, the doors at the back of the room slammed shut. Someone wandered out to introduce the night's special guest speaker, "Bakas's own true messenger, a real fire-and-brimstone orator . . . " For some reason that drew a laugh.

And Max looked up to see Michael, walking out of the shadows and up to the podium. He looked gaunt, all the soft light gone from his face, drawn into eyes almost red with a fiery intensity. He was wearing a black shirt, black pants, and black motorcycle boots, as were the two men who flanked him. No jewelry, Max noticed.

"Brothers," Michael began, and Max realized this was an all-male crowd. "Brothers, the Apocalypse is upon us, and we have only to make our choice. Do you want to be a part of it, or be its victim?" He talked about the angel who rode the back of the devil, from whom he apparently received his marching orders. "Would you ask Death who he prays to?"

Max smirked; Michael had stolen that line from him.

The deal was simple: Michael and his followers fed the beast, and the angel protected them from harm. There was one catch: the food. Apparently the beast craved pain, and to show you were worthy of protection, you first had to submit to intense suffering. If you didn't die, you were saved, and became one of AA's inner circle.

Between thumb and index finger, Michael held up a circular black pill, the "donut of death," as Max had once called it. So, at some point, either in prison or on the street, Michael had figured out what Terry was really doing, and now had co-opted that role. What if I had just told him when I first found out myself? Max thought. Could I have saved his career? And did he remember—

Well, apparently he did, because Michael was looking directly at Max as he announced that a special celebrity acolyte was about to Take the Test.

"I heard he was coming to town, and left him a personal

invitation."

Doh, Max thought. No one's more devious than a cop.

"Everything I am today, I owe to this man," Michael said, indicating Max. "Years ago, before I found my calling, I was a sinner without purpose." There were disapproving mumbles from the congregation. "I was a sinner without purpose, *and* a cop." The mumbles grew substantially louder. "But this man *gave* me a purpose. I had a family, I had a career, but all I wanted was him!"

Max tried to share a look of healthy skepticism with the stone-faced crowd.

"And through him, I found the doorway down to the truth! I was sent to prison, not a pleasant place for a former Officer of the Law." Some of the congregation sniggered quietly at this. "It was a place of pain, a place of *great* pain! But it was pain with a purpose!"

Max found it disquieting that the audience really, *really* seemed to approve of great pain.

"I lay in my cell at night, bruised and sorry and alone. But I was *not* alone. Something else was there, something I might easily have overlooked, something right there, living in the prison with me. Your eyes play tricks when you've been in the dark, in solitary for days, don't they brothers?"

A number of AA members knew and agreed.

"So you don't trust your eyes, even when they're *not* tricking you, even when they show you the truth. As I am going to show you the truth this evening.

"I woke up, night after night, with a cloud over my head, and thought I was going mad. People *talk* about a cloud over their head, but I *saw* the cloud. If I watched long enough, I saw it get a little bigger, change a little, as when a snake swallows a rat. It would settle on my chest, and go to sleep." He paused, paced briefly. "I had no one to talk to, so I talked to *It*. And you know what I talked about?" He pointed directly at Max. "I told it about you!"

The audience was silent. Michael spoke only to Max now. "There was something that made me love you, and yet made it impossible for you to love me back. I wanted to know you more than I ever wanted anything, but there was something inside you that was unknowable.

"I thought to myself, I'm lying here in this house of pain, giving my pain to something, why not ask something in return? So I asked it about you. And you know what, Max? It knew you! It knew you, Max."

There was dead silence now. "The Shadow that lived in that prison, that fed off our pain, was a personal friend of yours, Max. But it wasn't so fond of you anymore. It told me you had betrayed it, just as you'd betrayed me.

"Welcome home, Max," he said in a flat, unreadable tone, and he held the pill above his head.

Max thought of saying something like, "Honey, I've come back to you," but he knew his crowds, and he wanted to get out of this place in one piece. And besides, the pill was just high-grade Ecstacy, wasn't it?

Wasn't it? The two henchmen came for him, one on each side of the row. Max stood and joined Michael at the podium. Embarrassed, he held out his hand, and Michael gripped it firmly, and Max saw that his old lover was missing a finger.

"Open your mouth," Michael said, and when Max complied, Michael inserted the pill. Max nearly gagged, but had to swallow when a thick red liquid was poured into his mouth, something along the lines of Chateau Dracula 1876.

"Jeez, I'm not a helpless puppy," he sputtered, dribbling blood as the two henchmen lifted him bodily and strapped him to the altar. He was already getting woozy. His tolerance for drugs was high, and he was pretty sure there wasn't a pill made that could have gotten into his bloodstream this quickly. Something in the drink, then?

An enormous numbness settled over him. No, *not* a numbness exactly, he could feel the cold stone against his back, the bruised pain at the back of his head where it had flopped against the altar as he was dropped onto it. He could smell the collective sweat of the thirty or forty men in the room and a peculiar, rank smell that seemed to emanate from the altar itself. But he was incapable of moving a muscle. His shirt was stripped from him, and then his shoes, pants, and underwear.

Max was not pleased to note that one of the henchmen was offering Michael a selection of cutlery from a lacquered black case. He tried to read Michael's expression, but could not, and couldn't speak either, couldn't speak to ask an urgent question: what was that part about *if* I survived the test? He couldn't even hold *that* thought in his head, nor the following one, which had something to do with his fully understanding the depth of Echo's disability. Something was pressing down on his head—no, on his mind, something he had never experienced before, something almost like a heroin rush, blotting out every other thought and sensation; except there was no pleasure in this, as if the pleasure that should have been rushing between his brain enzymes and his gut were being drawn off, siphoned somewhere else.

The shadows on the ceiling were roiling like fast-moving clouds before a storm, when Michael cut into him. The pain was exquisite. With each little cut, Michael would step back, show the bloody scalpel to his audience, pause for something that didn't occur, mumble something about the impurity of his pain, and then cut again. Max tried to scream, but only a gurgling sound came forth. All his energies were being focused through the pain itself, pain building, reaching a threshold beyond which he could not contain it; and he felt it seize his body in one all-embracing convulsion. He opened his eyes into a complete darkness, seeing not the room around him but something else, somewhere else entirely, a world without corners, without depths, bottomless.

And he felt the presence of Juno. Felt her astonishment at finding him here, her repulsion. He was sure that it was she who made him pass out, pass out just as the doors crashed open, their sound miles distant, yet immediate, and the last thing he remembered.

25

Epigrams are as pointless as sex.
—Max

The first time he actually remembered being awake after what he swore was going to be his last AA meeting, Max saw Echo sitting on the end of his bed. Couldn't be a hospital bed, he realized, because it wasn't annoyingly high off the floor. And the walls weren't some shitty pastel shade, one of those colorless colors that probably helped your eyes adjust to being dead. They'd put him in a damn nice hotel. A suite, actually.

"Am I staying with you?" Max asked Echo.

"No," Roberto replied, from a chair on the other side of the bed. "Your friend is still at large, and I won't permit her to stay anywhere near you while he is. He probably doesn't know where you are right now; your medical treatment has been strictly private."

"So what kind of shape am I in?"

"Not bad, now that the drugs are out of your system. The damage done by the knives was inconsequential. A lot of blood, but not life threatening except for the shock you seemed to be in. Apparently the drugs you were given did that. Among other things."

"It felt a lot worse than that," Max recalled. "Would I have died if you hadn't shown up?"

Roberto shrugged. "I saw you when you were across the street from the park; had someone follow you. The place where you ended up, it had a bad reputation, so my man came back and we took a team down there. I doubt anyone from either side is going to call the police about the damage."

"It was Michael," Max told Echo. "He's head of some cult. I think it's affiliated with the Bakas people. He's making human sacrifices for Juno and her new pet." He looked out the window, and was momentarily startled; he could see half of Los Angeles from his bed. "It's another one of those dimensional creatures, but apparently this one only eats *bad* vibes. It's not hard to figure out why it likes Echo Park, although maybe Terry attracted it first by sending his victims into its dimension. Chummed the waters without knowing there was a shark around.

"I went upstairs, to the old apartment," he added. "The black figures: there are more of them, but they've moved. The two that used to be on the floor next to our bed are curled up in fetal position."

Echo looked at him so sadly he could hardly bear it.

"I'll be okay as soon as I get some sleep. Really."

"You've been having nightmares," Roberto informed him.

"I'll be okay now. Thanks."

Roberto escorted Echo out, speaking a few words to someone in the living room of the hotel suite.

Max dreamt he was looking into a pool of his own blood. Strangely, he didn't feel as if he were bleeding to death. It was more like the pond in the park, so much blood it would have had to come from a thousand people, from Max and all his ancestors, everyone he had known, from everyone who had drowned here with his dreams, every wasted life. He bent over the blood pool to try to sense its depth, and saw something, distant at first. A body? A dead body? It grew, rising toward him, face first . . . His own impossibly handsome face.

His own face, but somehow different. Max reached for it, reached toward the surface, even as his unmirror image reached for him. He plunged his hands into the blood, yet somehow the other Max eluded his grasp, their hands passing through each other.

But the vision remained in the rippling surface, and Max, studying the face, realized the eyes were gray, realized that the features, which he had assumed were distorted by their liquid medium, were not exactly his, but his and . . . Echo's. He felt an effusion of warmth coursing from his blood-engulfed hands up through his arms and then throughout his entire body, warmth like nothing he had ever felt.

And then the other face contorted, pulled away from him, and Max lunged forward in panic . . . and found himself crouched on the floor next to his bed, panting.

And, perhaps, understanding.

The backdrop was an enormous blowup of the picture of them Echo had saved from their first photo shoot, the one of Max blowing his bad boy pose because she was trying to crawl up his pant leg. Overhead, enormous black cables hung like ominous snakes, restless in the breeze. Max couldn't help thinking the stage looked like a gallows.

The police had had to cordon off the area just so it could be set up without interference from the locals, who seemed intent on either making off with the lumber or dwelling underneath it. At least it couldn't help but look better in the dark. If the concert was to save this place in any normal sense, he figured, they'd have to earn enough for terra-forming.

He hopped onto the stage from the front and briefly surveyed his kingdom of broken trees, torn shrubbery, trampled earth, and rubbish. *His kingdom*, because he didn't feel like wandering any more. He imagined Terry, in his place, would say something about Sisyphus finding meaning in his rock rolling. That's what Terry had been trying to teach him, he thought: you can't take meaning from something without first giving it.

"Want to change places *now*?" a voice said from beneath him.

"Terry? Damn, is that you?" Max tried to peer down through the cracks in the stage, but the planks were too well fitted.

Laughter was the only response he got, but it sure sounded like Terry's laughter. He jumped back off the stage and lifted the apron. He couldn't make out a thing under there, and when he called Terry's name again, there was no answer. A trick of the imagination?

He hopped back on stage and exited through the back curtain, down the stairs and directly through a black cloth tunnel to the performers' tent. A bunch of hospitality people were there, offering Cokes and sandwiches; also tech people, the press (of course), and neighborhood liaison types.

And Echo. This might be *their* reunion, but it was *her* show. She was checking out her bubble, or at least a model of it. The real thing was ten feet high and wouldn't be delivered until the last minute, when a crane would place it on stage with the audience already present. The crowd would be half-thinking it was just some hologram, or that, if it *was* Echo, that the bubble was designed to hide the fact she wasn't really singing. But she'd show them.

She froze when she saw Max. And then he embraced her.

"Hey, I've got a new song I think you're going to like."

"New song?"

"Wrote it for you. Just for you. Nobody but you and I will ever sing this."

"It's that bad?" Daniel snorted, entering the tent and clapping Max on the back.

"You'll see," Max said, certain he could fly one more time. "It's called, 'Different Lives.'"

Echo listened, professionally intent, yet increasingly disturbed behind that, and joined him on the second chorus:

There are different lives than those we lead,
And different worlds than we conceive,
There are rooms in which the voiceless talk,
and wombs in which the unborn balk
at every choice.

When they finished singing, Echo grabbed him by the front of his t-shirt.

He looked down for a moment, as confused as she was. "Maybe my real curse is that I can't *see* what love is about. I don't know if I can be different, Echo, but I just saw someone I want to be in love with."

She shrank back. Max rushed forward and grabbed her. "Why didn't you tell me?" He had tears in his eyes, but he was smiling.

She hadn't seen the smile in a long time. "Tell?"

"That you're pregnant. That you're going to have our child."

She looked at him in guilty confusion.

"It's true, isn't it, Echo? I don't know how you did it—well, I guess I know how, I just don't remember when—I mean, no offense—forget that. Just tell me, is it true?"

She smiled and nodded, and now she was crying too. They held each other.

"I saw him in a dream," Max said. "He's so beautiful."

"Beautiful?"

"Don't worry, he looks like you too," he laughed. "His eyes are so gray, and they reach right out to you. He touched me with those eyes, Echo. He's going to be wonderful. We're going to be . . . " He couldn't finish the sentence without

wondering if he were lying, wondering if, just by not fin-
ishing the sentence, he were implicitly bullshitting her, leaving her to imagine more than he could truly promise. He
closed his eyes fiercely and tried to believe he could believe.

As the hour of the concert approached, the sound crew
were having the same problem Max and Echo had experienced years ago in Las Vegas, feedback that sounded like
tires trying futilely to hold a curve. Echo sang it back from
her booth backstage, but Max could see she was distressed. It
was never long before another screeching trip around Dead-
man's Curve, and groans from the frustrated roadies.

Art, thought Max, is work. It's like flying, but not the
effortless soaring of an eagle; it's pumping your arms like
crazy just to stay a few feet off the ground, hoping you'll
grow wings.

Then he thought, I have wings. Echo and I have wings.

Behind the stage, the performers' tent looked like a Star
Wars attack center. Even the tent itself was made of a metallic
alloy fiber that was supposed to filter out the atmospheric
static Max and Echo had expected the creature to generate.
While it was only partly effective, they were glad for anything
that might interfere with Juno's awareness, awareness Echo
felt increasingly as the sky darkened, until she finally retreated
inside the crystal bubble they had constructed for her.

Daniel paced, the synthesizer woman impatiently smoked
Marlboros, and Max stared at his guitar, his fingers a quarter
inch from the strings, his thoughts on the face in the blood,
the face in Echo's belly.

The city allowed only twenty thousand people in the park,
but Echo's crew had mounted speakers on buildings for a
mile in every direction of the concert. The video cam and TV
guys were screwing with the erratically pulsating lights on

stage, and the crowd was barely controlled. Roberto had established himself in a bullet-proof metal tower in the middle of the crowd, where he had his own security command post, in constant radio contact with fifty men on the ground, about a third of them armed, contrary to LA city ordinances. From that vantage point, Max imagined, he could probably see all of the hundreds of thousands of people crowding the streets around the barricaded park. Everybody in the crowd, like everybody backstage, was restless. It was a live TV broadcast, and they had to start on time.

But Juno couldn't wait.

As the sun disappeared below the horizon, red-hued shadows fell across the park. The crowd began to rumble. And then Echo, in her crystal bubble, started to hum. The programming hadn't begun, and the TV producer looked at her like she was crazy, working when the camera wasn't on, but she began scatting the song she had sung to the creature in Las Vegas when she was drawing it toward her. Max, who was waiting at the back of the stage, sitting on a wooden step and smoking a clove, *heard* her singing before he *saw* her singing, and he sat a moment, paralyzed by memory, by beauty, by hope and loss. Then he picked up his guitar and walked out on stage. Daniel grabbed his sticks and gestured to the keyboard player, who hurriedly stamped out her cigarette butt with her knee-high vinyl boots, pulled her leopard spot dress down over her butt, and pumped both fists into the sky. The video cam guys gave gleeful fingers to the live TV crew.

Max started with a guitar lead some people might have recognized from the Days of the New tune "Real." The musicians jammed on it for three or four minutes, Echo scatting around it with her creature tune, but occasionally coming across with one of the song's actual lyrics. "Nothing's real, but it's real if you want it to be." The electric clouds above roiled in confusion, but more and more resolved into a face that had been seen a half dozen times over Echo Park in the past months. As the song reached a quiet crescendo, Juno was looking down at them.

"You're faced down, so turn around," Echo sang.

The live TV broadcast cut in, with the announcer whispering, too near the mike, "The fucking thing is listening to the music!"

"What if it doesn't like it?" someone else said.

Roberto, in his security tower, saw a lot of black-clad people in the audience. He had no moral conflict with profiling, but black was a Goth thing, not just AA. It was reasonable to expect Goths at this concert . . .

Max took the band into the song they'd been planning to open with, one of their originals from the first album, "Terry's Song," and Echo's image now appeared on the curtains behind the rest of the band. Fans who knew the song well, knew she—or someone—was singing it live. Max made a few abrupt dips and stops that had Echo laughing in the middle of the song. But where the hell *was* she? Five minutes into the broadcast, Max could imagine the TV producer already having a fit: "Is she going to come on, or not? This is billed as her first live appearance in three years!"

If Max hoped playing "Terry's Song" would conjure the old man, well, it didn't, but it put Terry's feel in his blood, and he gave the Juno cloud his best "fuck you" grin. Then he started into the new song he'd written for Echo, "Different Lives."

The images of Juno in the sky and Echo on the screen seemed to engage each other. Even the TV producer couldn't help noticing; it took him a few seconds to realize that the giant sky crane was finally lifting Echo's crystal sphere into the air. He went from a very brief orgasm to worrying that the audience would riot if they thought this was some kind of trick, just a hologram and not the real Echo inside the bubble—even though that was exactly the sort of doubt he had wanted to create. Back before he saw what Echo's fans looked like.

The announcer started yammering something about it being a diamond egg, that Echo and Narcissus were being reborn. *Where do they get this crap?* Max wondered.

As the crystal sphere began descending, the audience roared; those outside the park roared a moment later, and Max looked up to see the shadow creature briefly mirroring the image of Echo landing on the stage.

Roberto, in the tower, was on all secured channels at once, talking to his ground force. A band of a half dozen black-clad men were gathering into a nasty little knot he didn't like the looks of, suspected were AA. Twenty yards from the stage, the invading group saw the security team, and Roberto no longer had any doubts about who they were.

As the first chorus ended, just when Max might have been expected to rage into one of his, okay, *legendary* guitar solos, he stopped completely, as did the rest of the band, and Echo launched into a mind-blowing response to the creature's awful agony, screaming, wailing, thrashing with her voice. And *then* she hit the high note.

The shadow cloud, now part Juno and part Echo, was descending toward the stage, was within twenty feet of it, was about to cover half the immediate audience, when Echo hit the note, the high, piercing note, held it, held it . . . until an engineer surreptitiously pushed the button the FX guys had rigged to shatter the "crystal" sphere.

Roberto's eyes were on the AA group, and as tiny fragments of the bubble rained on the stage, he saw one figure in the middle of the group raise a pistol to shoulder height. Realizing with a horrible satisfaction that the improbable—but planned for—was happening, he pulled up his own scoped rifle.

Max was standing, his silent guitar clutched in both hands, staring up at the split face of the cloud above him, when he sensed the commotion a few yards from the stage, saw a group of security men scuffling with a black-clad cadre, saw, in the momentarily protected center of the group, Michael.

Michael, smiling at him, but pointing the gun at Echo.

What happened next was broadcast live, but better seen from the video cam footage that was spliced and slowed down later. As Echo stepped forward out of the crystalline shower, the crowd roared, people throwing their arms into the air, overwhelming the struggling group of assassins and security guards. Michael's first shot was thrown wide, up into the cloud, where it punctured the image of Juno. By the time he was leveling his second shot, Max had launched himself across the stage, flying into the air a few feet in front of Echo. His arms were spread like wings when Michael's bullet hit him in the chest.

Michael's mouth dropped open, but only for a moment, only until his head exploded from the impact of Roberto's bullet.

Echo never flinched. She raised her fists to the sky and screamed a song at the cloud, a song no one had heard the likes of. The tenements around the park began to crumble in a crescendo of concrete and glass, and the shadow cloud collapsed into itself, vanished into its own blackness. Echo looked down at her Max, lying open-eyed on the stage at her feet, a brilliant light pouring out of his eyes, fine as lasers, up into the shadows above the park.

EPILOGUE

Parents ask many things of us, but in the end it is all one thing, that we survive them. Sometimes it is too much to ask.

—Max

"Max and Echo embodied the two contradictory obsessions of teenagers everywhere, to be totally unique and to be like everyone else," Lucy told *Rolling Stone* a few years later. "I knew Echo and Narcissus would be irresistible to American youth as soon as I saw them."

Echo looked up from the old magazine as four-year-old Maxie plunked relentlessly on a small synthesizer. His magic riffled the pages, made them hard to read.

The interviewer pointed out that Lucy's opinion was based on the way Max and Echo looked, not the way they sounded. As if looks hadn't driven music careers from Elvis to Britney Spears. But it was *worth* pointing out in this case—Max and Echo looked like sex and death, pleasure and passion, and loss, no matter what they were playing. Where Max alone might have been too arrogant, Echo delivered his message in voices that were somehow familiar, so the listener was more likely to conclude that, yeah, that's how he would have said it himself.

So that's what Lucy claimed to have known. But what had Echo and Max known? After Las Vegas, neither of them seemed to give a thought to not continuing on together, although, from that moment, that night, they both must have known that any life they might still have together was doomed. They were irrevocably bound together by that night, but the bond had nothing to do with living together in the real world.

Ironically, the creature she had banished with her scream at Echo Park was closer now to Max than she was, living as it did in some dimension where spirit was the only tangible.

"Come here, Maxie," she purred. When the child responded, she showed him the picture of his father. "Who does he look like?" Echo had thought about not allowing mirrors in her home, but had decided to pretend to be normal.

"Daddy?"

"Yes." Good, she thought, he hadn't said, "Me."

They took each other's hands and walked out the door of the beach house, down toward the ocean. Maxie jumped from one tidal ridge to the next, using his mother's arm like a bungee cord, laughing like kids are supposed to. Had she ever? Had Max? Echo didn't remember.

"Look at the waves, Maxie. What do you see there?"

"Water riding on top of other water."

"What else?"

"Daddy."

He gave the same answer whenever he described a cloud. The shadows he sometimes talked to gave him greetings from his father. She held this tiny hand, thought, *What he sees is a miracle, his Daddy riding the world in every wave.*

A miracle is being able to talk to your child, to love him, to be loved in return. She gazed out at the waves, hoping somehow he knew that, yes, he had done something even he could not deny was worthwhile.

Afterword

When my son Max was young, he refused to learn to read or write because that's what his parents and his older sister did. To convince him it might be worth the effort, I tried to interest him in telling stories himself. I envisioned him learning grammar and spelling while he worked out these tales on our computer. Instead, *I* sat at the keyboard, while my ten-year-old son paced the carpet behind me, dictating his stories. Almost all of them began, *After the horrible and gruesome death of my parents* . . .

I wasn't worried that he was planning something. Once you get over the initial shock, it makes perfect sense for a child's story to begin this way, imagining a situation in which he is going to have to fend for himself. It's the only way for a kid or a teenager, from Cinderella to Spiderman, to have a real adventure.

Max had some scary real adventures over the next nine years, his life twisting and turning in ways no parent might have anticipated. But he kept telling stories, and, after a while, writing poems, which were more entirely, fiercely, his own, and for which he began to win awards. The lines attributed to Max in this novel are his, written at an age that froze my blood. This novel, *Echo and Narcissus*, began as my re-imagining some of Max's characters, colored by my own fear and admiration, and remembering, always, that the most exciting thing about a child—or a character—is the things he does that you never would have expected. And so it is not surprising that this novel begins after the horrible and gruesome death of Max's parents.

Thanks to my friends in the Writers of the Future 2000 group who made some helpful comments on this manuscript. Special thanks to Dan and Jennifer Barlow for caring enough about this book to want to publish it.

Thanks to my daughter, Amanda, who appears consensually in other stories and is often my reader, and to her mother, Carole, my wife of thirty years, who cannot help appearing in my stories, whether she likes it or not, because she has been such an enormous influence on my life.

And thanks, of course, to Max.

—Mark Siegel

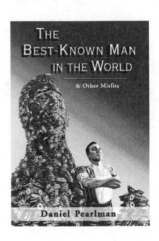

Mark Siegel . . .

was born in Buffalo and received his B.A. in Political Science from Williams College. He then earned a Masters in Creative Writing at SUNY Buffalo, where John Barth hated every word he wrote and informed him the Novel was dead. Mark stopped writing fiction for 20 years.

After receiving a Ph.D. from the University of Arizona, Mark taught American Culture in Japan. Later, he was elected chairman of the English Dept. at the University of Wyoming—an occurrence so shocking he immediately quit academia to fail as a part-time writer. At the urging of his wife and children, who did not relish the idea of subsisting on Ritz crackers and beans, he moved to LA and took a job with a highly successful developer as a consultant on things no one knew anything about. The firm moved to Phoenix, then collapsed a year later, leaving Mark to fail *full-time* as a writer. After a year walking the desert with a "Will Correct Grammar For Food" sign, he enrolled in law school at Arizona State. Since 1991, he has been a lawyer in Phoenix, where he lives with his wife of 30 years, Carole, and their children Mandy and Max.

Over the years, Mark has published a dozen books on subjects from literature to law, and finally, after a number of friends swore to him the Novel was, in fact, *not* dead, he again began to write fiction. In recent years, he has published the true murder chronicle *Rocky Point*, and 17 short stories. *Echo and Narcissus* is his first novel. He is worried, even at the age of 53, that his parents may find out and read it.